A typical Irish wedding

Gerard Byrne

Chapter One

Mattie Jenkins was a quiet unassuming man. He had worked most of his life on the building sites. Easily dealing with the large amounts of materials required to get each job done. Sourcing them, brokering the best deal for the company and then figuring out the logistics to get them delivered.

Any company that Mattie had freelanced for, had praised him to the hills and back. That's why it came as a shock to everyone when he suddenly announced his retirement from the trade. Choosing instead to go into the vending machine business. But not just any kind of vending machine. He figured that the most money to be made was from the ones in pubs and nightclubs toilets. Drunk people would buy any old shite when it was put right in front of their faces.

Unfortunately that market seemed totally monopolised at the time. But there was a slim opening. Mattie didn't bother with the usual stuff like run of the mill condoms, chewing gum and tablets to make your dick grow hard.

Hell no. That shit was for amateurs. Mattie decided to fill his machines with crotch less panties, posing pouches and other cheap sexy lingerie. Along with mini vibrators that he'd bought cheap in bulk online. His friends and family had thought he was mad. But the gamble paid off and his machines were a big hit. Emptying out after each weekend, as horny drunken men thought that the best present to bring home from the pub to your disapproving wife, was a cheap and nasty looking black thong, that had less material on it, than a strip of dental floss.

But Mattie didn't care about all those things. His business was booming. He had a few fellas working for him. So now he could finally enjoy one of his few hobbies that had been sidelined over the past few years. Magnet fishing.

Magnet fishing, for those who have never heard of it, is when you attach a heavy magnet to the end of a rope and you toss it out into a deep body of water and then slowly reel it back in. You only have to look on YouTube to see the popularity of the modern pastime. People do it all over the world and find the most amazing things. Swords. Cannon balls, gold, it's all out there just waiting to be found.

Unfortunately Mattie had never reached such heights with the bounty he'd gotten over the years. No gold, no antiques. Just a lot of crap. But he'd never given up hope and just moved onto somewhere else with some historical interest. This week his adventures had brought him to Meath. The Battle of the Boyne site, to be precise.

He had his Wellington boots on. Just in case he might have to go into the shallow waters to haul out any treasure he might find. But mostly he stayed on the bank, throwing his magnet out as far as he could get it, and reeling it back in.

He'd been told by people online, that the old canals around that area were a treasure trove just waiting to be found. Even on his arrival there that morning, Mattie spotted Spencer Cruise, one of his magnet fishing rivals, but also a good friend. The two men respected each other enough to give a good twenty feet in distance between themselves, as they both worked the same stretch of canal.

Spencer pulled his magnet up out of the water and found it was covered in rusty old nails again, "Jesus Christ. Only shite on this stretch", he started to pull the unwanted pieces of metal off his magnet, whilst discreetly glancing up to see was his friend doing any better, "you find anything decent yet?"

Mattie lifted the plastic box beside him and showed his friend the contents, "slow day by the looks of things"

"We're only getting started", Spencer replied, his natural giddiness flowing through him. Nothing excited him like magnet fishing. Not sex, drink or drugs could come near to the buzz he felt, when he threw his magnet out deep into unknown waters, in the hope it would bring back treasure of some description.

It was pretty damn easy for magnet fishing to come out on top. Spencer's sex life was null in void. Pity the same couldn't be said about his wife of thirty five years, Michelle, who in recent years developed a lust for big black cock. Spencer blamed himself for her new turn on. He'd brought her to a sex show in Amsterdam. It was all suppose to be a big laugh for them. Watching on as women stripped on stage or fired ping pong balls out of their nether regions. It was all going fine until this big muscular black guy came on stage. He was totally naked except for a truncheon that he held firmly in his hand. It was only then that Spencer realised that it was no truncheon.

The big black guy asked for a volunteer from the audience and Spencer's wife's hand had shot up from the crowd. Before she left her seat, Michelle had promised him that it was all a bit of fun. That quickly disappeared as the big black guy rubbed his abnormally big moist cock all over his wife's face. Slapping each of her jaws for good measure. Spencer had just watched on horrified as his beautiful Michelle seemed to be enjoying the humiliation. Thankfully it only lasted minutes and his wife reluctantly returned to her seat.

But the big black guy wasn't finished with his act just yet, as a small blonde naked woman came on stage and got on her knees in front of him. She obeyingly opened her mouth and let him fuck her face for what felt like forever. Holding onto her hair as if he was a professional jockey in the Grand National.

Soon the poor girl was exhausted and he lay her down on a big thick leather cushion and penetrated her in ways that poor Spencer didn't know possible. He had to look away a few times as things progressed a little too far for his liking, onstage.

But Michelle had seen things differently that day. Her eyes never leaving the stage for the whole of his performance. Things only got worse after they'd left. Firstly she had insisted on buying a massive black ten inch dildo. Then back to the hotel where Michelle started to pleasure herself on the bed with her new toy.

Spencer had tried to take part and satisfy his wife's new needs. Even attempting anal sex that night. But he couldn't keep up with her and soon he became just an unwilling spectator as his wife drilled her own asshole with the ten inch dildo. It had been a pretty grim holiday all round.

Unfortunately it didn't end there. When they had gotten back to Dublin and settled back into normal life, Spencer had started to notice his wife's new interest in using taxis all the time. Before Amsterdam, Michelle was happy to walk to the shops or take the bus into town. But now she was getting taxis everywhere. The next weird thing was that every single driver was black.

Spencer knew something was up, but chose to say nothing. Michelle was constantly in good form these days and she had started looking after her appearance once more. Wearing skin tight outfits and getting her hair done once a week. Younger men had started to take notice in her figure and Spencer didn't wanna be the one to bust her little bubble. No point in rocking the boat these days. Last thing he needed was for Michelle to leave him. Better to just turn a blind eye and let his wife get on with things.

Mattie fired his magnet back out into the water and gently pulled the rope back towards him. Straight away he could tell that there was something heavy attached to the magnet. He smiled over at Spencer, 'think I've hit the jackpot here. Something big on the end of the line"

"Could be another shopping trolley", Spencer had already found a few over the years.

"No way this is a trolley. We're too far up from the town for that. This is definitely something else", Mattie kept his pace at spooling in the rope, to a very slow speed. He was petrified that he'd lose his prized catch. And if it fell off the magnet, it would be pretty damn tough to find it again.

Mattie finally got his magnet to the edge of the canal and carefully lifted it out of the water. Attached to it was a big lump of muck and twisted roots. Whatever he'd found had been there a long time.

"What is it?", Spencer shouted up as he threw his own magnet back in.

"Not sure yet", Mattie started to wipe away the muck to find that the strange item was made of brass and that it seemed to be a cylindrical shape, "think it's an old used shell of some kind"

"What would an old shell being doing out here?", Spencer's magnet came up empty again.

"No idea", Mattie tapped the side of the shell, in the hope that all the mud trapped inside would fall out, but nothing was coming out. He turned the shell around in his hands and quickly noticed that it had never been fired. He glanced over at Spencer, "this is actually still live"

"You what?", Spencer wasn't sure what Mattie said.

But Mattie hadn't time to reply, as the shell in his hands exploded.

Spencer watched on as parts of his friend flew everywhere. There was this strange red mist in the air, where Mattie once stood. Then there was silence. It was as if all the animals in the area had decided to stop making their natural sounds out of respect for the dead.

"Mattie?", Spencer put down his length of rope and approached the area, where his friend once stood, with extreme caution. Scattered around the grass and narrow adjoining footpath were bits of flesh, clothing and internal organs. There was no definite one piece you could point at and declare that it was definitely Mattie.

Spencer wasn't sure what to do, so did what most would do when in a blind panic. He rang emergency services on his mobile phone, "hello, I need help. My friend's been blown to bits by something. Think it was an old artillery shell"

"Where a-bouts is he?", asked the strangely soothing female voice on the other end of the line.

Spencer glanced around before answering, "he's kind of all over the shop", there was even stuff hanging off the hedges and nearby trees.

"I meant where a-bouts did the accident occur?"

Spencer finally could see his mistake, "oh right. Sorry about that. I'm actually near the entrance to Oldbridge estate in Meath. Along the canal way next to it", he glanced around at all the blood and gore on show, for about ten feet in all directions, "trust me. You can't miss it"

Chapter Two

O'Dwyer's café was packed as always. It was one of those overpriced places in the city that attracted the more elite members of Dublin society. You wouldn't find beans on toast or a full Irish fry up on the menu. Just fruit salads, yogurts and a selection of exotic nuts to go with your overpriced black coffee.

Sophie had found a quiet booth near the back. Even better when she noticed a full length mirror built into the wall across from her. She could admire her new short blonde hairdo. Sophie's natural long red hair had been doing her head in recently.

It wasn't because of the colour, as most people thought. Sophie was quite happy to be red. But when you're an identical twin. It can get a little bit annoying when people always point out how similar you both look. The new haircut was gonna blow all that out of the water for awhile.

Sophie had always a strong bond with her sister Ellis. Yes there mother pushed that a little too much with matching outfits throughout their childhoods and well into their teens. Didn't help with the names either. The jokes never ending in secondary school about them being named after a faded pop star, whose biggest hit was about one night stands. When they'd complained to their mother Nancy. She'd just laugh and tell them that Sophie Ellis Bexter had a lot more big hits than just that one song. Murder on the dance floor being one of them.

Sophie's phone began to ring noisily in her handbag. She took it out quickly and answered. Knowing already from the flashing screen, that it was her fiancé Zara on the other end, "heya. How's work?"

"Pretty slow today", Zara pleasantly replied, "think there's still people giving us a wide berth since all that food poisoning last month"

Zara worked for this rather fancy restaurant called the Golden Slice. They prided themselves on the cuts of meat they used in all their dishes. Importing from many exotic countries to get the rarest of meats for their customers. You could chow down on kangaroo, crocodiles and even giraffes. Critics said it wouldn't last. But Dubliners had flocked to the restaurant and were more than happy to part with their hard earned cash.

That was until a major case of food poisoning broke out and dozens of customers ended up in casualty, shitting and pucking out of different orifices. One poor woman was caught short in the middle of Henry street and shat herself in front of horrified shoppers. The streaky yellow shit just ran down the inside of her short skirt and dripped out onto the red brick pavement like some kind of fucked up Jackson Pollock.

Tabloids and news websites were quick to point the blame at the Golden Slice. The restaurant was forced to shut down and let all their staff go for a few weeks while an investigation was carried out. But in the end it turned out to be none of the meats. It was all down to an egg fried rice that had been made elsewhere by a failing company who had been letting their standards drop in recent months. But shit sticks and the restaurant's good name was in tatters. Very hard to rebuild a good image, when you've got headlines in the tabloids like, "RESTAURANT OF DEATH" or "MAKE MINE A RUNNY ASS"

"Are we still doing this tonight?", Sophie was nervous about their plans for that evening. She could feel the sweat on her back as she thought about it.

"You getting cold feet again?"

"I'm just a little unsure of what to expect"

"It's all gonna be fine. Stop worrying and leave the rest to me"

"Okay", Sophie preferred it when Zara took control. She always knew what to do and say. The rock to her pebble.

"Has Ellis showed up yet?", Zara hadn't much time for Sophie's sister and didn't try to hide it very well. Not even when in her company.

"No sign of her yet", Sophie's eyes were still scanning the busy café for her sister. Only woman to recently arrive in the door, had short blonde hair. Not much different from her own.

It was only then that Sophie recognised the woman as her sister Ellis, "for fuck sake", she blurted out down the phone.

"What's wrong?", asked a concerned Zara.

"Ellis has got the same bloody haircut as me. I don't fucking believe this shit", Sophie could still see her sister at the counter, buying a coffee and some weird looking salad. She looked up and noticed Sophie watching from a distance and waved wildly. Sophie waved back, as she tried to mentally absorb what was happening.

"No way she knew you were getting your hair cut. Has to be a coincidence", Zara was always the type to try and think things through carefully.

Sophie tried to act normal under the distressing circumstances, "it's the same colour and length. That can't be a coincidence"

"Calm down hun and just breathe. Let your body relax and think happy thoughts", Zara was attempting her old yoga teaching voice again. One of her failed attempts at self employment. But no one wants advice off an instructor who is bigger than her own customers.

Zara hated her full framed figure. Especially her large ass cheeks. But that's what Sophie loved about her most. Burying her long tongue between her lover's large firm ass cheeks and probing Zara in places were no one else had the joy of exploring before.

"I'm fucking calm", Sophie sipped at her lukewarm coffee, "but should I say it to her out straight?"

"Just play it by ear. Sorry, but I've got a customer. Better make an effort to get the public back in. Talk to you later. Love you"

"Love you too", Sophie loved to say those words. She'd missed out on that emotion for most of her teens, as she tried to hide her sexuality from everyone, including herself. Her friends had thought she was taking her Catholic faith a little too far. Refusing to even kiss fellas on most nights out. The only person who knew the truth was Ellis. Hard to hide anything from your twin. A strong wooden raft in a sea of confusion.

Sophie put the phone away and tried to put on a brave face as Ellis approached. The closer she got, the more she could see how similar their hairstyles actually were.

"I see great minds think alike", Ellis sat down in the seat opposite and took her jacket off.

"Was going for something totally different. Marco said that this look would suit me", Marco being their rather flamboyant hairstylist for the last five years.

Ellis's face lit up, "that's who did my hair as well"

Sophie already had her target for a good bollocking, when she finally caught up with the little pink haired wanker.

They chit chatted for a bit and ordered more coffee. Both of them avoiding the elephant in the room. That was until Sophie couldn't take it anymore and blurted it out, "did you confront Steven about the silk leggings?"

Ellis had found them under the driver's seat of Steven's car a month ago and had been afraid to confront her boyfriend of two years about it. Sophie was even willing to swap places with her sister for a few hours, just so that she could come down hard on Steven. Something her sister wasn't good at. Especially when it came to men. Ellis was just a doormat to most of them.

"Yes", Ellis was growing more uncomfortable with this line of questioning. She was well used to her sister's controlling behaviour and want to punish any boyfriend of Ellis's, that slightly wronged her. Even the lovely James was bad mouthed for months because he tipped a waitress, even though the service was appalling. Sophie had accused poor James of fancying the waitress. When Ellis looked back on her love life, her sister seemed to be the continuing reasons why her boyfriends left her.

"And what did he say?", Sophie couldn't wait to hear the bullshit that Steven was coming out with. He was a user and the sooner her sister could see that, the better.

"He says they're his"

A brief silence fell over both of them. Sophie had to run that sentence over in her head a few times and still it didn't sound right, "what do you mean they're his?. Is he trying to say that he's a cross dresser now?. Because that's total bullshit"

"I knew you wouldn't understand. Steven pleaded with me not to tell you. He doesn't want this getting out"

"Bet he doesn't, the lying little toe rag", Sophie was frantically searching her mind for a clear cut way to show her sister that all this was bollocks, "have you seen any other stuff belonging to him, like dresses and women's underwear?"

"No, he doesn't want me to see him differently. Says that he's upset enough that I found the leggings"

"I bet he's fucking upset alright"

Sophie sat back in her hard wooden chair and studied the weak and fragile face on her sister. Hard to believe that at one point their personalities were so in tune. Telling them apart was nearly impossible to most. Then fellas came along and fucked all that up. Trying to show Ellis the light was getting harder and harder, "who's the Saint of lost causes?

"Saint Anthony", replied a bewildered Ellis. She was already sensing that her sister was about to unleash one of her long winded narratives.

"That's who you should be fucking praying to all the time. You're a lost cause to me these days. I'm not even suppose to be getting stressed at the moment, and I meet up with you and already I can feel my heart rate going ninety. When I hear all the bullshit you put up with off men, it makes me so fucking happy that I never went near them from the start"

Ellis wasn't taking this lying down, "fuck you and your mightier than thou attitude. You only ever wanna hear the bad about my love life. You always shut your ears to the good stuff. Never heard you once taking an interest in all the holidays that Steven has brought me on. We went to Disneyland Florida only two months ago and you didn't even comment or like my photos online. Everyone else did. But my own sister couldn't even take the time to at least show her interest in my life. I'm always there for you and Zara. I'm so happy that you've finally found love. But lately I feel like you've been pushing me away, and don't give me any more crap about Steven, because me and you both know that isn't the true reason. You've got a problem with me and I wanna hear it now"

"Only problem I have with you is that you keep becoming a doormat for men", Sophie was starting to raise her voice. She couldn't give two shites about who heard her in the busy café.

"And what about Anna?", Ellis fired back, while trying to not let her eyes get drawn to the large television that was mounted on the wall above her sister's head. There was some news story about a bomb blast in Meath. The place looked familiar.

Sophie hated to be reminded of that name, "what about her?"

Ellis leaned over the table and kept her voice low, out of respect for her sister, "she used you like a personal piggy bank and was seeing other women behind your back"

"There was no solid proof in that", Sophie fired back.

"There was. It's just that you can't be bothered to accept what everyone else was telling you. Even mam caught her out that time"

"Don't bring mam into this. She only gives a fuck about herself and where next to spend dad's money"

"That might be true", Ellis let out a much needed breath of air and tried to calm down a bit. She hated fighting with her sister, "but that doesn't mean it didn't happen"

Sophie had heard enough and started to gather her stuff together, "don't know why I even bother to build bridges with you all the time. Now you're even siding with mam these days"

"I'm not siding with mam. You're only saying that because you hate to hear the truth. Besides, you're with

Zara now. All that shit from the past is not important. Why can't we talk openly about it for once?"

Sophie stood up and grabbed her jacket, "the past is the past and that's where it should stay. Don't get why people are so obsessed with dragging it up all the time. Why can't it just be left where it god damn is"

But Ellis wasn't listening. Her eyes transfixed on the television above her sister.

Sophie found herself getting even more angry, "now you can't even be bothered to listen to me"

Ellis was still lost for words as tears began to form in her eyes. She just pointed at the television above her sister. Sophie turned and looked up to see a picture of their father on the screen. The accompanying news article was about an explosion out in Meath. There had only been one fatality. Their poor old father Mattie.

Ellis stood up from her seat, with tears rolling down both cheeks. Sophie dropped her jacket and bag and hugged her sister tightly into her. All their relationship problems quickly dissolved into nothing. For now they were two lost souls again.

Chapter Three

Margaret had always found it amusing that her name and phone number was written up on the men's toilet wall in her local pub Murphy's. With the obvious added tag line, if you want a good time ring. Thirty or forty years ago, Margaret would have found such graffiti offensive. But now it came as a sense of pride, to think that men of all ages, wanted to be deep inside her.

Just like now as Rickety Rick dipped his withering stick, into Margaret's well pummelled fanny. There once was a time when being bent over a piss wet toilet seat and taken roughly from behind, would have be a degrading situation. But now it felt like a badge of honour. Men still wanted her and wives and partners who were ten or twenty years younger than her, feared that Margaret might set her sights on their man. Many called her the black widow since a few men had died in her bed. But you've gotta expect that when you sleep with a lot of older men with dodgy hearts.

Take Rickety Rick for instance. Seventy nine and soon to pass onto the big eighty. Bald as a plucked chicken and still wearing clothes that were fashionable thirty years ago, for funerals and court appearances. His wife had been dead eight years and he lived alone. His kids had all fucked off to the furthest corners of the earth. So all this poor fucker had was Murphy's pub. And the only women he ever got to talk to was the ones that haunted the bar most nights. Sitting on the high stools with their reddened knees exposed and wearing high heels that were normally badly scratched and discoloured.

That's why Margaret couldn't help but give the old fucker a sympathy fuck. But there was a little incentive in it for her, "don't forget Rick, you promised me a pint for this"

"I'll buy you two Margaret, if you let me spank your ass a little", Rickety Rick wheezed loudly as his lungs struggled with the unexpected workout it was now taking part in.

"Go on then", Margaret was always surprised at how kinky some of these old fuckers truly were. They'd look all quiet and nice, when you met them out in the real world with their kids and grandkids. But get them alone and the filth that would pour out of some of their mouths even shocked Margaret at times. One of them even offered to eat the shit from her asshole. That might sound all great in the porn world, but when it's pacemaker Larry who runs the church choir down the road, it kind of just comes off a tad sleazy.

Rickety Rick gripped her sides tightly, "I'm fucking about to blow", he wheezed loudly.

Margaret gripped the back of the toilet and struggled to keep her knees balanced on each side of the bowl. It was much easier before someone tore all the feckin seats off, "just go for it Rick"

He happily complied and began to spank her thick wobbly ass happily. Reddening the cheeks more and more with each hard slap, "fine little thing you are. Taking my good eight inches like that"

Margaret would have argued that it was more like six. But no point in busting the old man's bubble while he was about to reach the peak of ecstasy for men of his vintage. She was far more concerned about the smell of Deep Heat that was emanating off the old man's body. Rickety Rick must have been covered with the stuff. Thankfully he hadn't asked for a blowjob.

Rickety Rick finally shot his load, before falling against the bathroom door. He struggled to ease his breath back to what he would have considered normal. He gulped in large breaths of air as he held onto his weak old heart.

Margaret dragged herself, with much difficulty, off the rim of the toilet, and soon seen the distress that he was in, "calm down Rick, calm the fuck down", she put her hand over his chest and tried to slow down his rate of breaths by apply some mild pressure at the right time. All the time trying to speak soothingly, "just try to breathe normally. Where's your inhaler?"

"At the bar", he blurted out through gasps for air.

"Wait here and I'll be back in a minute", Margaret sat him down on the toilet and unlocked the door. Thankfully there was no one listening in this time on her sexual shenanigans. It had become some kind of fucked up tradition for the other men to sneak into the toilets when she was satisfying one of the locals.

Margaret rushed through the rest of the poorly kept toilets and out into the bar, which always had the look of a place that would have happily belonged in seventies Ireland. All cheap wooden counters and poorly matching furniture. Thick curtains hung on many of the walls, hiding the dreaded daylight from everyone inside.

There was a few regulars sitting around the place. But none seemed to take an interest in Margaret grabbing Rickety Rick's inhaler off the counter. They were all to busy with the horse racing on the telly.

That was all except Bernard, who was sitting further down the bar with his best friend Rory. They'd always been inseparable over the years. Pity the same couldn't be said for their marriages. Both of them on the wrong side of fifty and chilling out after another long day on the building sites.

"Please don't tell me you killed poor Rick?", Bernard wasn't even joking. Wouldn't be the first time that the black widow had took a life.

"Fuck off Bernard", Margaret hadn't time to get into it right now, as she rushed back towards the toilets.

"What's going on in there?", Rory asked, his eyes still glued to the telly.

"Think Margaret has killed Rick?", Bernard replied, his eyes now wandering back to the telly.

"Well at least he died happy"

"True"

Margaret rushed back into the toilets and stuck the tip of the inhaler in Rick's spit covered mouth. She began to frantically press the button, releasing the life giving gases down his throat.

A few seconds later, Rick started to catch his breath once more, "thank you so much. Don't know how I'm ever gonna repay you for this"

"You can start by buying me three pints instead", Margaret replied.

Soon after, Margaret escorted Rickety Rick back out to the pub and sat him down on his stool, "time to get a bit generous with those three pints now"

"Is that the going rate these days?", Bernard loved to wind up old Margaret. Didn't bother him that he'd been balls deep in her himself, a good few times over the years.

"Fuck off you", Margaret fired back half jokingly. Better to not show her annoyance. Only fed their remarks even further.

Rory was fidgeting with the buttons on his phone as he tried to open up a news story without the added pop up ads and buttons to sign up to email updates. It wasn't going well, "fuck these stupid phones"

"What are you trying to do with it?", Bernard enjoyed watching his friend struggle with technology, even though he wasn't any better with it himself.

"Trying to get up this news story about a bomb blast near Drogheda"

"The natives must be getting restless again", Bernard joked, "they're like a mini Belfast up there. I was talking to a guy from Derry awhile back, and he said that he wouldn't go near the place, and he's from a fucking war zone himself"

"It's not that bad anymore", Rory gave up and put the phone down on the bar, "they only shoot the odd person these days"

"They should put that on the tourism posters", Bernard waved his hands aloft, as if imagining the poster in his head, "come to Derry. We kill less people these days"

"Not exactly catchy", Rory went back to nursing his pint. It was already getting warm.

Suddenly a shaft of sunlight shot in the door, as it was pushed open by two young women. Both had long blonde hair and were wearing shorts that barely covered the cheeks of their asses.

Bernard was up off the stool like a shot, "hello young ladies. Are you lost by any chance?", they had to be, to wander into one of the diviest pubs in the city centre.

One of the blondes swung off her backpack and placed it on the table next to her, before fixing her extremely tight T-shirt that showed more cleavage than a contestant on Love Island, "we are looking for the Guinness brewery", her accent was European of some type. But Bernard couldn't care less where.

"You walked by it already", Rory didn't even turn away from his pint on the bar, "you need to head back the way you came for about fifteen minutes"

"Thank you very much kind sir", the blonde picked back up her bag and headed for the door.

Bernard panicked as he tried to think of something to say to stop them, "fancy having a drink with us?. I'll buy you a pint of Guinness each. Start off your tour on the right foot"

The blonde smiled, "thank you very much for the kind offer, but we are in a big hurry", and with that, the two blondes rushed out the door and the shaft of light vanished once more.

Bernard threw his hands up in disbelief as he walked back to his stool, "what's wrong with you?. Two young fit birds come into this place. Something that never fucking happens in this dive", he noticed old Marion was listening in from behind the bar, "no offence love, but you know what I mean"

Marion just ignored him and went back to her telly.

"I'm available if you wanna buy me a drink", Margaret had been ease dropping on their conversation. She hadn't much choice since Rickety Rick was still struggling to talk.

"I'm not that desperate", Bernard was well aware that things could change as the day went on.

"Your loss", Margaret replied with a cheeky smile.

Bernard turned to his friend and lowered his voice for once, "this is not fucking like you. Me and you used to be going around pulling loads of fanny. Young and old. Tight and wide. Diseased and the squeaky clean. We've fucked it all. Like a team. The A fucking team. That's what we feckin were. We didn't let marriage or kids get in our way. Only a year ago we'd be both balls deep in those two pieces of crumpet that came in the door"

"Crumpet?", Rory finally looked up from his pint, "since when have you started describing women as crumpets?. Think that slang died out a hundred years ago. We're both like fucking dinosaurs these days. Young women look at us like we're old"

"Speak for your fucking self", Bernard was slightly deluded at how well he was ageing. He liked to think the grey streaks in his hair were go faster stripes and that the growing bald patch at the front was a solar panel to power his roaring sex drive. When in fact it was pretty much fuelled by viagra and cocaine, "I've still got the body of a model"

"Yeah, a model Ford cortina", Margaret shouted down from her stool.

"Fuck you Mags", Bernard fired back, "I'm trying to have a private conversation here"

"The other day I was walking down the street and I tripped on a pothole", Rory was still trying not to smile at Margaret's last comment, "went down pretty hard on my knee and I was trying to get up when this really hot red head came over and put her arm under mine. I mean this girl was Black Widow good looking"

"Thanks very much", Margaret announced.

"Not you", Bernard fired back, "he means the real hot red head one from the movies", he turned back to his friend, "please tell me I'm right?"

"She looked the spit of the movie one", Rory cupped his hands in front of his chest, "her boobs were massive and just resisted gravity something shocking. I could of gotten happily lost in that cleavage and never wanted to be found"

"Can't really see were you're going with this story, because it sounds fucking awesome already", Bernard was already getting a horn as he imagined shooting his load over that red head goddess that he could never think of the name of.

"It was that look in her eyes. Like a professional carer tending for the needs of an elderly person. There was no lust or chemistry in those beautiful blue eyes of hers. Just pity. I never felt so old in my whole fucking life. She even helped me to a nearby bench and sat me down. Those beautiful tits in my face the whole time. But rather than get a semi downstairs. It just shrivelled up instead. I'm fucking losing my edge with the ladies. Never thought I'd see this day happening. I'm not even sixty for god sake"

Bernard put his arm around his friend's shoulder, "tell you what. Why don't me and you go out on the pull tonight with a big bag of coke and a load of hard on pills, and go pull some tight fit fanny. What do you say?"

It was then that the horse racing took a break and a newsreader appeared on the telly. Beside him was a picture of a familiar face. Most of the punters in the bar went quiet as the full news story was read out with little emotion from the newsreader.

"Who the fuck would blow up Mattie?", Bernard had known the man for many years, when they'd all worked on the building sites in the old days. Mattie had been kind of like a father figure to him.

"You wouldn't know these days. Wrong time, wrong place kind of shit", Rory had fond memories of the man himself. Mattie had been great help in getting Rory's own building company off the ground in the early days.

Margaret was sobbing over her fresh pint from old Rickety Rick. She'd been married to Mattie for eight years in the early part of her life. Her first and only love, "my dear Mattie", she sobbed, "bet that bitch finally had him murdered", the bitch part referring to Mattie's second wife Dolly. A woman who sank her claws into Mattie when the money started to roll in from the vending machines in the late nineties.

Rickety Rick tried his best to console Margaret, "now, now dear. You shouldn't be thinking the worst like that. Could have been just some kind of terrible accident. Doubt his wife got him murdered"

But Margaret was adamant who the culprit was, and even a landslide of evidence wouldn't deter her from her way of thinking.

Chapter Four

You kind of feel like you've missed something really
eventful when you find a jet ski in your film reel shaped
swimming pool. But this was Beverly Hills and Marcus
had seen a lot of weird shit here in his seven years in
Hollywood.

He missed the days of being a big fish in a small pond.
Everyone knew his name back in Ireland. Another Irish
comedy drama from Marcus Jenkins. His name sold the
movies alone. Didn't have to be his biggest hit. People
would still flock to the cinemas and the money invested
in the product would be made back within a few weeks.
No one complained and everyone would walk away
happy.

But Hollywood was a lot different from back home. The
producers were like vicious sharks who wanted their
pound of flesh and another ten like it, for good measure.
Marcus's screenplays were subjected to endless rewrites
and major plot changes. Even his cliffhanger endings
were too complicated for most of the Hollywood execs.
This kind of shit wouldn't happen back home. He was
gonna give it all up five years ago. Then Heavenly
Celeste arrived on the scene.

Heavenly Celeste had started off her time in the
limelight as a wannabe rapper. Even wearing baggy
tracksuit bottoms, which were so low that her dental
floss style underwear was mostly on show. Strangely
enough, it became Celeste's trademark and she'd

regularly shake her booty at most of her sold out concerts.

But people soon bored of her mediocre rap lyrics and her attempts at being gangster. So Celeste tried her hand at acting. Unfortunately she was wooden as fuck and no one wanted to work with her. Well, no one that had any self respect for themselves. So Celeste slogged around in some low budget comedies and even did an extremely unerotic sex scene for a so called up and coming director, who disappeared quicker than he arrived. But the sex scene stayed in the public's thoughts. Even being constantly parodied and sneered by different American comedians for the next two years. Celeste was at her wits end. That was until Marcus appeared on the scene.

Marcus had been invited to one of these so called major Hollywood parties. But Marcus always seen it as the same shit, just on a different day. He'd been hiding out beside the oversized swimming pool, with a large statue of a naked woman in the middle. Water cascading down her marble body and finished up in the pool. Great to look at, but unfortunately there had been a number of concussions when drunk visitors had swam into the base of the statue, in the poorly lit pool.

Then out of the darkness, Heavenly Celeste had appeared, wearing a short latex dress that had more holes in it than a teabag. She was crying and attempting to light up a joint. Marcus, being always the gentleman, had made himself known, before lighting her thick reefer. They had talked that night. She'd admitted that her career was going downhill and fast. That every producer in Hollywood had decided she was septic and it would be suicide to work with her.

Marcus had always found a strange attraction in the vulnerabilities of a beautiful woman. He so wanted to help Celeste that night, that he threw caution to the wind and offered to write her the perfect leading role in a film that would have to be done on the cheap, but would still be powerful in itself.

Celeste had jumped at the opportunity and even paid for the movie production out of her own pocket. After just six weeks of shooting they came out with the finished product, THE EYES DON'T LIE. A dark psychological thriller about a young prostitute, played by Celeste, dealing with her growing plastic surgery addiction. It was a massive hit and won many awards all over the world. Unfortunately Celeste missed out on the best actress Oscar that year. But suddenly everyone wanted to know her again and quickly she grew closer to Marcus and soon they were married.

Unfortunately, like most Hollywood marriages, the cracks started to show pretty quickly and Marcus found that their lives were travelling on two very different tracks. They barely seen each other anymore. He was working on new projects off the back of the last one, while Celeste released new music and took parts in other gritty dramas.

So it was a bit of a shock when Marcus arrived back to find their house in the hills, totally trashed. There had been some kind of food fight in the kitchen and living area. Whipped cream had been sprayed all over the tinted glass walls on all sides, and it looked like someone had rubbed their body parts into it. There was even the perfect creamy outline of someone's large breasts and pound coin sized nipples. Marcus would have put money on it that those breasts belonged to Celeste's best friend and partner in fashion crimes, Tory Summers. A popular porn star who tried to reinvent herself as a lingerie designer. Unfortunately there wasn't much call for crotchless panties and leather bras with the metal studs on the inside.

Marcus walked into the bedroom to find clothes scattered around the floor and the bedsheets thrown all over the place. It definitely looked like someone had been having a lot of fun in there without him. It was then that he could hear laughter and giggling coming from the bathroom.

Marcus pushed open the door to be hit with a face full of steam. Piles of foam had poured out all over the floor. But none of that mattered, as his eyes focused on the naked gyrating bodies of Tory Summers, his beautiful Celeste and some extremely tall fella with the body of a young Sylvester Stallone, but it was more his twelve inch penis that caught the eye first. Especially when Celeste and Tory were taking turns and sucking it, while the other would suck his hairless balls.

"What the hell is going on?", Marcus was trying to sound aggressive, but he still felt pretty intimidated by the large muscular man in the room, and his oversized erection.

Celeste wasn't even bothered by the interruption and left Tory to deal with their steroid induced friend, as she stood up out of the steamy waters. Foam stuck to her body in all the wrong places, "we talked about this last week. You agreed to us having a threesome"

"That's because I thought I was going to be involved in it in some way", Marcus was still finding it difficult not to look at Tory sucking on the man's shaft, like he'd been bitten by a poisonous snake and she was poorly attempting to extract the poison.

Celeste brushed back her long wet pink hair out of her face as she climbed out of the oversized tub and put her arms around her upset husband, "now that you're home, it can be a foursome. We can all explore each other's bodies together"

Marcus was still trying his best not to look at Tory deep throating the stranger, but his eyes kept getting drawn back to it, "I never wanted this threesome in the first place Celeste. I'm happy with our sex life just being me and you. I just agreed to Tory joining us because you kept going on about it. Now you have some naked guy here, with a penis that looks like it was grown in Chernobyl"

"The name's Chad", the naked guy waved over at Marcus as he controlled Tory's bobbing head with his other hand.

"Nice to meet you Chad", Marcus was a bit lost at what else to say to the naked man getting head in his bathtub.

Celeste grabbed Marcus's hand, "come on in and have a bit of fun"

But Marcus gently pulled his hand out of hers and backed away, "think our fun days are over Celeste. I'm just gonna go get my stuff and get out of your way", he was internally kicking himself the whole time. Marcus so wanted to exploded and start smashing stuff. Maybe even roar some abuse at everyone in the room. But where would that get him?. Just a sore throat and a head full of guilt.

Marcus couldn't help but be confused by the sad face on Celeste as he shut the bathroom door behind him. It was like he was the bad person. That he'd been the one to wrong her. He'd even took a mental image of her naked body one last time. Just incase he struggled to remember her beautiful figure in the future. Those perfectly placed tattoos on her back. Symmetrical in all the right ways. Her hairless tight vagina. Something that didn't come natural. Celeste regularly paid for a procedure to make her feel like a virgin again. That was all great until you found out her asshole was looser than a middle aged woman, who had ten kids by natural birth.

Two hours later, Marcus found himself at his assistant's apartment complex on the other side of town. It was the only place he felt he could go at such short notice. The building was pretty old fashioned with its thick brick walls and wooden balconies. He pressed the buzzer a couple of times and waited for an answer.

"Who is it?", asked a woman with a rough Scottish accent.

"It's me Carla. Can I please come in for a bit. Don't know where else to go right now", Marcus felt more lost in Hollywood than usual.

The thick security door opened and Marcus wearily plodded up the overly lit staircase to the adjoining landing. Carla was already standing in her open doorway wearing oversized shorts and a black T-shirt. Her short multicoloured hair was tossed around like she'd just gotten out of bed.

Carla only had to take one look at her boss's face to guess what was wrong, "take it you didn't return to a happy home?"

Marcus made his way inside her apartment and sat down on her surprisingly hard couch, "arrived home to find my wife having her planned threesome without me"

Carla sat on the arm of the couch and lit up a joint, "who was the other players involved?", she took a few drags and handed it to her boss.

Marcus gladly took it. He needed something to drown out the emotional pain, "Tory and some guy named Chad. Guy was hung like a donkey. I mean he was that long, you could have used him as a pole for hanging jackets on, in a nightclub's cloakroom"

"Sounds like my kind of guy", Carla replied with a glint in her eye. Her sex life since moving to Hollywood, had been quite colourful. Sleeping with men, women, transgenders, transsexuals and any other alternative sexual lifestyles she could find. Her parents had always told her that variety was the spice of life. Carla just took that to a whole new sexual level.

"Please don't start", Marcus pleaded, "haven't the head for jokes today. I knew things weren't working out lately. I seen the cracks in my marriage. Celeste is still a young woman and probably has needs I can't fulfil for her. I never should have asked her to be my wife"

Carla sat down next to him, "Celeste is younger than me for god sake, and I even think you're too old for me"

"Feck off you. I'm only five years older than you", Marcus was starting to doubt whose side his assistant was on.

"Actually six"

"I was near enough"

"Not near enough for my liking"

Marcus's phone rang loudly in his pocket. He tried to ignore the annoying ringtone that he had recently selected to piss off everyone on the movie set. It was that stupid Crazy Frog tune from years ago.

Carla tapped his phone bulge, "answer it. Might be Celeste wanting to apologise and work things out"

Marcus pulled out his phone to see that it was just his mother trying to get in touch after god only knew how long. Probably looking for money and some help with paying off debts. She seemed to be of the opinion that because Marcus lived in Hollywood, that he was suddenly a millionaire. That couldn't be further from the truth. A lot of his own money was reinvested back into future movie productions and he'd signed a prenup agreement with Celeste, when they'd gotten married. Now Marcus hadn't even a home to wallow in self pity in.

Marcus ignored the call and put the phone back in his pocket, "haven't the head for my mother right now"

"Thankfully I don't have that problem with my mother", Carla replied.

"That's because she's dead"

"Exactly"

Marcus's phone rang again. It was still his mother. He internally debated if it was important enough to answer.

"Maybe it's important", Carla tried to coax him to do the right thing.

Marcus bit the bullet and answered the call, "hi mam. What's wrong?"

Marcus listened on for a few minutes as his mother babbled on through tears of anguish, before finally telling her he'd be home as soon as humanly possible. Then he hung up the call and fell back on the couch like a man who felt truly defeated in all that he had tried to achieve in life.

"What's wrong?", Carla sensed the worst already.

"My father's dead", Marcus couldn't believe he was saying those words out loud.

Carla put her hand to her heart, "oh dear god I'm sorry to hear that. Was it a heart attack or something?"

Marcus just stared up at the ceiling, "no, she said that he was blown up by some kind of explosive device. The guards are still investigating it"

Carla was lost for anything supportive to say, except, "fucking hell. Bet that hurt"

Chapter Five

Gary opened his tired eyes and stared up at the badly kept hotel ceiling above him. The place was pretty divey, but cheap for the illicit affair that he had been happy to take part in for the last two years. In his own opinion he was doing no wrong. Aisling was his ex wife and they had eight wonderful years of marriage, until he started fucking her younger sister Wendy behind her back. Thankfully neither of them found out about the time he skewered their mother Betty. Surprisingly enough, Betty had been quite fond of the anal fun, unlike her two daughters.

Aisling had gone on to marry again, had three more kids and she even found time to forgive her wayward sister. But like her first marriage, boredom sank in. Just this time it was from Aisling, who by chance bumped into her ex husband at a party one night and their budding affair commenced. Now it had just become a chance for them to release all their stresses on each other and just enjoy a bit of pillow talk.

"Penny for your thoughts?", Aisling still had her arms wrapped tightly around his midriff. She wouldn't dare boost Gary's ego by admitting how much she missed these tender moments between them. Her husband Edwin was a good father and worked all the hours of the day, but that didn't leave much time for them to play husband and wife. He spent more time back in England, working on business deals for his family's company. At first Aisling hated how distant they had gotten in recent years, but lately she was using the free time to enjoy life a little more.

"I think Edwin might have paid someone to follow me", Gary couldn't shake this growing feeling that there was certain characters on different days, watching his every move in public.

"Don't be so silly", Aisling playfully pinched his right nipple, "you're only getting a little paranoid. That's totally normal with what we're at these days"

"But Edwin is gonna catch us sooner or later. Maybe he's planning ahead for a divorce"

Aisling lay onto her back and whipped the covers off to expose her naked body, "does this take your mind off your worries at all?"

The sight of Aisling's pink bits on show, sent a tingle down to Gary's semi erect cock and it quickly stood to attention like a dutiful soldier whose angry sergeant had just entered the room. Gary's mind was still filled with concerns, but for now they were cast aside as he climbed onboard the ex wife express and brought her wet pussy for a much needed ride around ecstasy street. His eyes still darting over to the clock every so often to check the time. He had places to be that evening and things to do.

Suddenly, Gary's phone started to ring on his bedside locker. He ignored the growing ringtone and carried on ramming his sensitive cock into Aisling's wet pleasure hole. But each time the phone stopped ringing, it would start again as quickly.

"Someone's keen to get in contact with you", Aisling dug her nails into his back as another orgasm shot through her tired body.

"Just ignore it", Gary kept on thrusting as the sweat dripped off his forehead onto his ex wife's breasts.

"Fuck me you horny cunt", Aisling arched her back in the hope of receiving better penetration.

Suddenly Gary couldn't hold back his load no longer and it shot deep inside his ex wife with much relief. Then that pang of guilt once more, as the realisation that he hadn't worn a condom again, hit him hard. Aisling kept saying it was okay. But it felt far from it.

The phone was still ringing on the locker and Aisling couldn't help but investigate the identity of the caller. She picked it up and answered without asking Gary for permission, "hello, you're through to Gary Jenkins used cars and van hire. How may I help you?", Aisling had put on her best phone voice. Kind of a mixture between her own accent, and her posh sounding husband Edwin.

She was soon listening carefully to the emotional rantings of a distraught Margaret as she broke the bad news of what had happened that morning in Meath. Aisling couldn't listen to any more without guilt starting to grow deep inside her and handed the phone to Gary, "it's your mother"

Gary reluctantly took the phone and listened to his mother sob loudly through her bad news. He jumped out of the bed and started pacing the hotel room, listening to everything his mother had to say, while regularly telling her that everything was gonna be okay. It wasn't long until he'd hung up the phone and collapsed down on the floor beside the bed.

Aisling wrapped her arms around his shoulders from behind, "your mother said that someone's been killed in Meath"

"My dad was blown up by a bomb or something", Gary couldn't believe he was saying those words out loud.

"A bomb!. Jesus Christ Gary, that's terrible", Aisling hugged her ex husband even tighter and began to kiss his greying head in different spots.

"Don't know why I'm feeling like this. Always wished him dead for the way he treated my mother over the years. Casting her aside when that Dolly bitch appeared on the scene. I know he paid for everything me and Marcus needed, for years after that. But we needed a fucking father, not a bloody piggy bank", Gary pulled Aisling's arms tighter around his naked body, "he walked away from us and never looked back. Now I'll have to go to his bullshit funeral and listen to all these people I don't even know, talk lovingly about my father. Don't think I can face that"

"You have to go. He's your dad", Aisling so wanted to be there for her ex husband, but wasn't sure how.

"He was my father in name. That's about fucking it"

"But you still must have some good memories of your time together as a child?. Even just something small that stands out in your thoughts right now"

"There's nothing", Gary replied, while driving back the past from his thoughts, for fear that it might cause him to cry. Something he had been good at suppressing his whole life.

"I can go with you if you like", Aisling didn't see any harm since Edwin couldn't complain about her going to the funeral of someone she knew. Even if she couldn't remember the last time she'd met Mattie. He'd definitely showed up a few times in the early years of her marriage to Gary. But her ex husband's attitude has driven an even bigger divide between father and son. Mattie had been trying to build bridges, but Gary just kept knocking them down. Unable to forgive his father for the way he treated his first family. That hatred had only intensified over the years.

"Don't even know if I wanna go myself", Gary could feel his anger bubbling up once more, but he fought hard to keep it under control.

"You have to go", Aisling replied, "your mother needs you, and so will Marcus. The pair of them try to act all strong and that nothing can get to them these days, but you and I both know that it's all an act"

Gary didn't give her a reply, but he knew his ex wife was right. His family needed him and he couldn't let his own hatred get in the way. Not for now, anyway.

Chapter Six

The Jenkins family home was built up high in the Wicklow mountains. The locals had been delighted at first when it was announced that part of the building was going to resemble an old fashioned castle wall with a drawbridge that stretched out over a wide heated moat, filled with a variety of exotic fish. That was until it was painted bright pink. When you walked through the gates, you felt like you were entering a gapping vagina.

Unfortunately for poor Sophie, that feeling never subsided, as she drove her small car over the drawbridge and parked it next to her mother's pink Aston Martin. It was a hideous looking car with its pink interior and fittings. And the amount of times it had been keyed while out in public was mind blowing.

Ellis was still crying in the passenger seat, still unable to accept the news about their father, "he can't be dead. I was only talking to him yesterday"

Sophie got out and walked around to help her sister. It was times like this that she hated. Always having to be the strong one for them both. When was her moment to break down and be comforted by others?. It never seemed to come her way. Forced to bottle up the pain once more and move on.

The mansion that sat inside the three sided castle walls, was totally different in style and taste. When you entered through the drawbridge entrance, you were actually arriving to the back of the house and main parking area, while the front was facing out to sea. It had a rather splendid garden separating the mansion from the cliff edge. Thankfully they didn't have to worry about erosion since they weren't right up on the sea. A nice little beach below, kept the waves at bay.

Sophie and Ellis made their way through the tacky household until they arrived at their mother Dolly's special room for going out clothing. Dolly had built up that many items over the years that she needed somewhere specific to keep them. So Mattie had gotten his games room turned into a long corridor with large pink wardrobes on either side. Dolly had loved it. Especially the rotating shoe rack on one wall.

When the two twins stepped into the overly lit room, they noticed that their mother was trying on a dark purple power suit and high heels, and was now admiring herself in a full length mirror, in front of their put upon house keeper Collette.

"I could definitely pull this off at a funeral", Dolly held her stomach in as tight as she could. She'd been slipping up a bit lately with the carbs, "what do you think Collette?"

"It's beautiful Mrs Jenkins", replied a mousy Colette. Poor girl was all skin and bones. And her pale skin left Colette looking like she was lacking in the right vitamins at the best of times.

"I thought so to", Dolly turned her hips slightly, so that she could admire her own ass in the mirror, "really shows off my best qualities"

"Can't believe you are trying on outfits when dad is lying on a coroner's slab somewhere", Sophie sat her distraught sister down on a small pink couch inside the door, but stayed standing herself. She wasn't letting her mother get the upper hand.

"Trust me dear", Dolly was still checking herself in the mirror, "doubt your poor father is on any coroner's slab. They picked the poor man up with buckets for god sake"

Ellis wailed loudly upon hearing this.

Sophie fought back the mental image of gore soaked buckets from her thoughts, "don't say shit like that. Ellis is struggling enough already and here you are, already planning the perfect funeral outfit. I know you and dad weren't close anymore, but could you at least show a little bit of compassion. And why didn't you ring us before it was plastered all over the news?. We didn't deserve to find out like that. Especially not Ellis"

Dolly finally turned to face her daughter, placing her hands on her surprisingly thin hips and swished her bleach blonde hair out of her face, "what about me?"

"What the fuck about you?", Sophie was already sensing that she was about to get a big, poor me, sob story off her mother.

"I'm the one left to deal with all this. Planning a funeral isn't easy. There's flowers, the coffin, where to have the afters. That lot has to be done in the next few days", Dolly turned back to the mirror to admire herself once more, "Collette my dear, please can you go get me a glass of Prosecco"

Collette jumped up from her seat, "right away Mrs Jenkins", before hurrying out of the room with a strange fast paced shuffle of the feet.

Sophie noticed through the reflection in the mirror, that there was tears in her mother's eyes, but were quickly wiped away. It might have been a small indicator of grief in most people, but Dolly held back her emotions so much, that to show even such a small sign of weakness, was a big fucking deal. Sophie's mother was hurting, and dealing with the situation in her own way, by being an even bigger bitch than normal. It was only at that moment that Sophie finally realised, where she got her own stubborn and hard hearted personality from.

"Look mam, we're all hurting in our own ways. But it's better for us to pull together at this difficult time", Sophie hoped by forcing her mother to answer a question about her father's death, that it might dislodge some more much needed emotional outbursts, "was there anymore about how dad died?. They said it was an explosion"

"That stupid hobby of his. Wouldn't listen to me when I told him that it was a waste of time. Didn't think it would be the death of him. Honestly, how can an old live army shell, sit at the bottom of a canal for decades and never explode. Then your poor father comes along and blows himself up with it. The guards reckon that the magnet activated something inside the bomb and it began to tick down. Your poor father had enough hassle trying to turn me on. Looks like he hadn't that problem with the bomb"

"Please mam, I don't need that mental image", Ellis had been in a world of her own until she heard her mother over sharing again. But she had more pressing problems weighing down on her thoughts, "do you think they'll let us go see the place where dad died?"

"Not for a good while sis", Sophie rubbed her sister's back gently. It was something that calmed down Ellis over the years, "they have to make sure the area is safe. The army reckon there's a strong chance that there might be other unexploded shells in the area"

"Do you think Marcus, Gary and their mother knows what happened?", Ellis had discreetly tried to build bridges with her brothers in the past. She had met Gary for lunch a couple of times, and they had shared details about each other's lives. It had helped both of them fill in some gaps.

Marcus on the other hand was a harder person to get a hold off. Always busy making new films and television shows. If Ellis was brutally honest, she wasn't a fan of his work. Too dark and dreary for her liking. She'd left numerous messages with his agent. Even Gary had left Ellis's details with Marcus, but to no avail.

"I don't give a fuck if they know or not", Dolly spotted Colette swishing back into the room with a silver tray, topped with a bottle of Prosecco on ice and three champagne glasses. But Dolly just grabbed the bottle, popped it open and started drinking it off the head. She cleared a good third of the bottle before coming up for air, "he's our Mattie, not there's. No fucking way. If that Margaret one gets her chance to make a scene, she'll be well in there in front of all our friends and family. Fuck it. I'm gonna get bouncers for the doors of the church, and the graveyard as well. That bitch and her kids aren't getting near the place"

"You can't do that mam", Sophie had no relationship with her two older brothers, but she wouldn't see them left out of the arrangements for the funeral. Though her views on Margaret were a lot different. She found the old woman quiet rude and nasty, the few times the had met over the years, "dad wouldn't want that and you know it. Please don't make the next few days more difficult than it has to be"

Dolly sat back down and mulled over her daughters complaints, before taking another large swig from the bottle, "they can come then. Your father would have wanted everyone at it", she paused in deep thought for a moment, "I really do miss him. I know we weren't that close at times. He had his hobbies and so did I. But he still knew how to make me laugh when I was feeling down. Pity he's not here now", and with that, tears started to roll down Dolly's cheeks, "I wish he was here right now with us"

Sophie and Ellis rushed over to their mother and both hugged her tightly. They may have been down one member of their family, but that didn't stop their own love from attempting to fill that invisible gap that had appeared amongst them.

Chapter Seven

A photo can speak a thousand words. Bring you back to a particular time in your life. Jog the tired old memories and break that thin film that has built up over the top for many years. Marcus was getting that sensation off the crumpled old photo in his hand. It had been taken one Christmas by his granny. In it there was him, Gary and mam and dad. Life seemed so normal back then. There was no shouting or fights between his parents. None that he could remember. So where did it all go wrong?.

Marcus put the photo back in his pocket and looked around first class. It was filled with mostly business types. All black suits and grey hair. Probably using the company expenses to pay for their luxury trip to Ireland. There was the odd lady in a suit as well. Marcus reckoned that the more attractive ones were probably the secretaries of the grey haired suited men, while the older and more ugly ones probably made it here on their own steam. It was the circle of life. Only the good looking and the toughest made it to the peaks of personal achievement, while the rest floundered around below.

First class definitely lived up to its name. Champagne, orange juice and sparkling water was constantly offered throughout the flight by stewardesses with supermodel looks and teeth so perfect that they could have gotten a starring role in a Colgate commercial. Even the one overly camp steward looked like he'd drop to his knees on request, if a blowjob was on the inflight menu.

Marcus reclined back in his oversized chair and tried to take his mind off things by flicking through the channels. He wasn't sure what was upsetting him most right now. His wife's regular infidelity with other men and women, or his father's untimely death.

Celeste wasn't aware that her husband had seen a lot more of her indiscretions over the years. Marcus had just tried to turn a blind eye to it. She was definitely more into women than men, but Celeste still seemed to feel the need to make out to the media that her marriage was perfect in every way. Marcus couldn't deny that his wife was a good laugh to be around and always made him smile with her weird jokes and messing around behaviour. The public rarely got to see that side of Celeste. Unfortunately she was more remembered for a sex tape that was released, were she had left a webcam on in her bedroom when she was nineteen, and filmed a rather erotic lesbian entanglement with this Japanese girl in one of their traditional schoolgirl outfits. It blew Pam and Tommy's honeymoon video out of the water with popularity. Who needs real dick action when you've got to lesbians and a strap on.

After he'd found a music channel playing songs by Heavenly Celeste, and a few of her movies on demand, Marcus gave up with the small screened telly and went back to looking around the cabin. Near the front of the plane was a well known actress called Dorothy Devine. She was well into her sixties, but to look at her you wouldn't think it. She was the original ageless beauty before Jennifer Aniston came along and stole her limelight. Even winning one Oscar for best supporting actress in a film that no one can remember the title of. It was one of those art house jobs that escaped the dungeons of video bargain bin rental hell and climbed the ranks to be noticed. The weird thing was that no one really went to see the bloody film. It was four hours long and most of it took place in one singular bedroom with Dorothy doing big streams of monologue to a brick wall. She had boasted for many years afterwards that she had memorised every word of those speeches, but there was always rumours that she cheated a little. But honestly, there would be no harm in that if she did. Dorothy had thick, large sunglasses on, leading Marcus to wonder if she was hiding more of the plastic surgery that she told everyone she never got.

Carla finally appeared back from the toilets with a big smile on her face. She was wearing a baggy T-shirt and those so called fashionable ripped blues jeans that looked like she'd been dragged behind a speeding car for half a mile. She plonked her body down into another first class seat that was a few feet away from Marcus.

"You took your time in the toilet", Marcus wasn't one to normally study the toilet pattern of anyone he knew, but his assistant had been missing a good half hour.

Carla tied her hair up into a bun, "went on a little dick hunt around the plane and came across this really hot fella from Texas. He has the big ten gallon hat and all. Asked him could I have it, but there wasn't a hope in hell he was parting with it"

"So I take it you joined the mile high club then?", Marcus was pretty sure that he was the one that was suppose to be getting all the sex, and that his assistant was suppose to listen to his risqué stories. Not the bloody opposite way round.

"I joined that years ago mate", Carla picked up her empty champagne glass and waved it around for attention, "need a drink after that", but there was no sign of a stewardess at that moment, so she gave up, "you can't say that it's not exciting"

"I've never tried it", Marcus sipped at his own glass of champagne, delighted that for once he wasn't the one left without.

"Yeah right", Carla sat up in her seat, "there's no way you've never tried it. All you Hollywood types do be at it, and even your Celeste is famous for getting off in plane toilets"

That was more of a scandal really, since she'd gotten off with the captain of a plane on a transatlantic flight. Didn't go down too well when they'd hit a rather large pocket of turbulence and rather than the captain going back to take control of his aircraft. He chose to stay in the toilet with Celeste and finish off their sexual liaison. Last commercial flight he ever worked on, but he said it was well worth it. Probably because he was selling that story to the press for years after.

"I'm just not into it. To me good sex is in a comfortable place were you don't have to be constantly concerned about being caught by other people", as the words flowed out of his mouth, Marcus couldn't help feel a little boring in comparison to his friend. Leading him to believe that maybe Celeste had a point in trying to spice up their sex life. Just a pity she hadn't waited for him. But the image of Chad's giant swinging dick still haunted him, like one of those creepy paintings that the eyes follow you around the room wherever you go. Women always said that sized didn't matter, but that always seemed like total bullshit when you seen the size of the cocks they craved.

"Comfortable safe sex is for all those lovey dovey couples who are obsessed with each other to the point of stupidity", Carla always had a way with words, "I'm talking about the sex you have with people who you don't even know the surname of. For fuck sake, I've even fucked people who I couldn't even tell what gender they were, let alone a first name. You're in your forties now and are starting to think like an old man. You don't seek out wild and carefree sex anymore. You're looking for security and all that shite, and if that's what you've set your heart on, then fair fucks to you. But unfortunately your Heavenly Celeste is not on the same weary tugboat as you. She's on the top of the range speedboat heading in the opposite direction. The sooner you see that, the better"

Marcus was a tad lost for words. Probably more to do with the fact that he still hadn't gotten used to getting a talking down from his own bloody assistant again. Thankfully there was no one around they knew this time to hear it.

"What's this father of yours like?", Carla had been trying to change the subject and the words were only out of her mouth when she realised her mistake, "sorry about that. I mean what was your father like?", didn't sound much different than the first time, but at least it sounded right.

"It's kind of awkward because I only have memories of my dad, after he left my mother. There's not much there before that. When you get a few beers into my brother Gary, and he's in the right mood, he'll tell you loads of nice stories about us all living together in our first house. My dad had used all his savings to buy the place out straight. Probably a hell of a lot less than what you'd pay these days"

"Ain't that the fucking truth", Carla muttered under her breath.

Marcus continued, "then my father started this toilet vending machine business and the money started rolling in. He quickly built up a pretty big business that drew a lot of attention of investors. Unfortunately when a bit of power came my father's way, his head started to turn to all the younger women that was sniffing around. My mother always says that my father started out as a good kind man, but it was the money that changed him more than anything. Young blonde women were suddenly a regular fixture on the small factory floor that he had bought on the outskirts of Dublin. There was rumours that he had been having affairs with a number of them, including that bitch Dolly"

"Who the fuck is Dolly?", Carla had been losing interest in some of Marcus's stories, but she was pretty sure that the name Dolly hadn't been mentioned before.

"Dolly is the woman who my dad left my mother for. My mam said she could have dealt with all the flings. She still loved my father and felt that sooner or later he'd come back into the open folds of the family and be as one again. But he was bewitched by that bitch Dolly and soon the truth came out. Bringing my mother to dinner in this fancy Italian restaurant and telling her over a romantic meal for two, that he was leaving her for a woman that was over twenty years younger than her. Then he drove her home. Turned out he already had his belongings in the booth and drove away. Now you can't say that it isn't a bit of a fucked up way to end a relationship?"

"I once dumped a guy and then jumped out of a plane", Carla replied totally deadpan.

Marcus wasn't sure whether he was being took the piss of or not, "fuck off. No way that happened"

"Yes way it happened", Carla replied with a cheeky grin, "his name was Martin and he was boring as fuck and stuck to me like super glue. Couldn't give this fucker the hint that I was getting tired of his boring ass and needed to move on. So he brought me parachuting one day. You know those ones you see were you're strapped to a professional. Well my guy was super fucking", Carla loudly kissed the tops of two of her fingers like she'd just had a wonderful meal, "the fucking muscles on him had to be seen to be believed"

"I'm sure they were", Marcus hoped that Carla would just get back on track with her story.

"I had the hots for him"

"Doesn't surprise me"

"And wanted to feel a little less guilty about chatting him up on the way down. So I told Martin it was over and jumped out of the fucking plan. Never seen him or his depressing little face ever again"

"And what about the fella you were strapped to?. Anything else happen with him?", Marcus wasn't sure would he regret asking that question.

"Turns out he was married", Carla replied with a bit of disappointment in her voice, "but we still had sex in the long grass that day. So a win win in my book"

"Your moral code is lower than a member of the Trump family"

"I'm not denying that mate", Carla kind of seen it as a compliment in a way, "I'm just not willing to settle for less than what I deserve, and you shouldn't either. Look at us both here on this fucking plane, in first class. That's a thought. How the fuck did you afford first class?. Thought the company was running on fumes these days"

"I'm using Celeste's air miles. She couldn't give a shite about collecting them, because she has so much money coming in these days, so I just hooked up my account with her busy travel itinerary and hey presto, I get free flights. And they're open ended, so we can fly back at anytime, first class"

A beautiful young blonde stewardess came over, whose name tag had Judy printed across it. She was super smiley and leaned down between Carla and Marcus to speak quietly, "there's just been a few complaints about the rather coarse language you are both using at the moment", she spoke with a really hot American accent that was leaning towards old school Hollywood, "we need you both to keep it down for the rest of the flight please"

Carla leaned back in her seat and folded her legs, as if trying to strike a pose, "I just can't help using that word when there's a beautiful woman like you in the area. That word just keeps running through my mind. Getting faster and faster the more I look into your stunning green eyes. It's so hard to control it now as I smell that wonderful perfume emanating off your well toned body. Tell me Judy, are you single by any chance?"

Marcus didn't know were to look as his eyes darted away from the car crash that was about to happen beside him.

Judy stood up with this weird confused expression across her face, as if she still couldn't believe what Carla had just said to her, before walking back up the aisle of the plane.

"She's hot for me", Carla announced proudly.

"I highly doubt that", Marcus wearily replied, "scared would be the first word that comes to mind. But honestly Carla, what do you get from fucking around all the time?"

Carla leaned over the edge of her big comfy seat, "you know the feeling you get when you've completed one of your movie projects?. When you can do no more and it's up to the punters to give their opinions on your work. That's the satisfaction I get from bringing all walks of life to a mind shattering orgasm. Men, women whatever, fall at my feet in a puddle of their own hormonal juices. They can't get enough of fucking me", Carla spotted the attractive blonde stewardess ushering her discreetly towards the toilets, "think I may have another happy mile high customer on the horizon. I'll talk to you in a bit", and with that, she rushed off up the length of the cabin towards the nervous looking blonde stewardess and soon they were both locked in the toilet cubicle.

Marcus couldn't believe what had just happened. He mulled over the words that Carla had used as a chat up line on the blonde stewardess. If any man had a tried a similar style, they probably would have been arrested by the Air Marshal for sexually harassing a member of staff.

Life had gotten too complicated for Marcus. He figured it might be a good thing that he was returning to Ireland for a bit. Life had to be a lot easier back there.

Chapter Eight

It had been a long day, but Sophie was still pumped up on adrenaline from dealing with her father's death. It just didn't seem right that such a good and caring man should die so horribly. Where was the justice in this world?. All those pedophiles, murders and rapists who got to die peacefully in their sleep, while her father was blown to a million pieces all over the side of a overgrown canal.

Life wasn't fair. It wasn't like Sophie had only recently come to that conclusion. She'd felt like this her whole life. Always feeling short changed. Questioning from an early age why she had to be the one who was into women?, why did she have to be the one with the weight problem?, and why did she always have to be the one to be strong for her family?. Now she had no choice anymore. The supporting beam of Sophie's family was now gone, and she had to take on the weight and pressure that was already baring down on her. Life was most definitely unfair.

Thankfully Ellis had wanted to stay with their mother. At least that was one less thing to worry about. Sophie couldn't handle a whole night with her mother making everything about her once again. Hard to tell how much she actually cared, with all the Botox. But Sophie could be sure that it definitely wasn't as much as she and Ellis were suffering. The twins had a strong bond to their father throughout the years. People always said that daughters naturally get on better with their mother. Not in this case.

Their father Mattie had always tried to make time for his little princesses. That's what he loved to call his twin daughters. Started off with their love of Disney. They wanted the long colourful dresses and dreamed about Prince Charming, or Princess Charming in Sophie's case, climbing up the side of a tall tower to save them. He'd helped feed their imaginations and gave them a life away from computer games and electronic devices. Something that didn't happen much anymore. He gave them time to be kids before the real world got a hold of them and wouldn't let go. It was only in the last year or so, that the twins could fully appreciate what their father was trying to do for them. Too little, too late.

Sophie parked her car up for the night in the fenced off area of her apartment complex. It was a development that her father had invested money in. Beautiful views of the Liffey and only twenty minutes from the city centre. The apartments themselves were a mixture of modern art styles and the latest electronic gadgets built in.

Personally, Sophie found a lot of the new technology was infringing on people's privacy. Most of her friends would be happy to give their personal information to a modern, fancy, smart fridge, just for the laugh of it, but Sophie wouldn't even dare share her details. Why would a fridge want to know her weight and height anyway?. That just didn't make any sense.

But of course her fiancé Zara was more than happy to share information with every electronic device in their apartment. She didn't have any hangups about technology and embraced it more than most people. Sophie wished she wasn't so uptight about everything. Just let loose for once. But that day would never come.

Sophie opened the door to their apartment with the fingerprint scanner device that she thought was way too high tech for a normal apartment building. The door swung open and she placed her heavy handbag on a nearby sideboard. It was always strangely heavy. Which didn't make any sense since there never seemed to be a whole lot in the bag.

It was then that Sophie noticed the smell of incense in the air. She looked down the corridor to see a number of colourful candles lit along the way. Suddenly Zara appeared in the doorway into the sitting room. She was wearing a long floral dress than clung to her large frame in all the right places, and her dark dreadlocks swung freely as she walked up to the woman she loved most in this world and threw her arms around her waist.

"I'm so glad you got home in time", Zara was still speaking over Sophie's shoulder as she kept on hugging her tightly.

"In time for what?", Sophie was still drawing a blank.

Zara broke off her embrace and stood back to see if her lover was joking, "Sebastian and Marco are calling up tonight, for the special night we planned"

"Oh fuck", was all that ran through Sophie's mind. She'd forgotten all about the plan for that night.

Sebastian and Marco were a gay couple who the two girls had befriended over recent years. Sebastian was originally from Nigeria and had come to Ireland to study law, while Marco was from Mexico and worked as a podium dancer in a rather popular gay bar in the middle of the city. Both couples really wanted a baby, but Sebastian and Marco struggled to find a cheap surrogate mother to carry their child. Turns out it can get rather expensive to have a child when you don't have a uterus. Sophie and Zara on the other hand, had two perfectly good uteruses, but neither felt comfortable about having an anonymous sperm donor injected inside them.

All this had led to a rather drunken discussion between the four of them, about how maybe they could all help each other out. Have one child between the four of them. Then they'd be able to share the work involved with bringing up a baby. Taking turns between the four of them.

But there was also another reason for the four of them to have sex. Even though they'd all had previous sexual partners. Sebastian and Marco had never once been with a woman, and Sophie and Zara had never once been with a man. They figured it might be more fun to try it the old fashioned way. At least that would mean that it was a gamble who the father might be, but also it would be a gamble who might end up as the mother. Both girls were at the peak of their pregnancy cycle. Something that had strangely happened over the few years they had been together. Sophie had heard of close friends changing to match each other's cycles, but she never believed it until now.

"You forgot, didn't you?", Zara was far from impressed, especially after all the work she'd done to get the apartment ready for that night.

"I didn't forget", Sophie couldn't believe that she was about to say those words out loud, "my dad's dead"

Zara was lost for words at first, "how?"

"Have you not been watching the news?. He's all over it"

"The guy that got blown up in Meath?"

"He was magnet fishing again. God only knows what he hooked onto. Guards reckon it was an old unused shell. But they're still searching the places for fragments of the device", Sophie regretted using the word fragments, as a mental image filled her mind of her father's body, splattered across a wide area of the countryside. She fell to her knees and broke into an endless stream of tears and runny snot.

Zara picked her fiancé up off the floor and guided her towards their cream coloured couch, which had been a present from Sophie's parents when they moved into the apartment. It wasn't hard for Zara to carry out such a task, as she was naturally pretty well built and was always able to handle herself in a crisis.

When Sophie was sitting down comfortably, Zara went to the kitchen to get her a rather strong drink. Something with a lot of alcohol and very little mixer in it. Sophie wiped her eyes and tried to pull herself together. All the time those regular few words kept running through her head, "you have to stay strong. Other people need you right now". She was now the level headed one of the family, and her mother and sister were going to turn to her at some point in the next few days and expect answers. Answers Sophie wasn't even sure she would be able to supply.

Zara came back with a glass of clear liquid and handed it to her fiancé with a gentle pat on the back, "drink this and it might take the edge off"

Sophie did as she was told. Gulping hard at the contents of the glass that quickly burned her throat back into reality, "fucking hell Zara, that's fucking Sambuca"

"You needed a strong hit to your system, and that was that"

Sophie nursed the glass in her hands, "how am I going to get through the next few days. My heads flying around already and my heart is going ninety every time I think about my poor father's death. He was a good man. He didn't deserve to die like that"

Suddenly the intercom buzzer roared into life. Zara wearily shook her head, "that'll be Sebastian and Marco. I'll go down and talk to them outside. Explain what's happened and that we'll try it another night"

Sophie realised that maybe a quiet night in with just her fiancé, wasn't the way to go if she wanted to force some of the negative thoughts out of her head. Maybe a bit of company was exactly what she needed. People she could trust, "let them in, but please explain to them that we won't be going through with the foursome tonight, but that I would enjoy their company at this difficult time"

"Okay then", Zara rubbed her fiancé's shoulder once more, before getting up off the couch and buzzed their friends in.

Sophie listened on as the two men arrived at the door and Zara poorly whispered to the pair about what had happened to Sophie's father. Soon the three of them came into the sitting room to join Sophie.

Sebastian looked like he just walked out of a business meeting with his shirt and pants combo. He had thick leather brasses on and a matching tie. He always had a habit of overdressing for college. Even his lecturers found it a little uncomforting that their student was better dressed than them.

Marco on the other hand was more laid back with his long strewn hair, ripped jeans and overly tight white T-shirt, that showed off all the bulges of his growing muscles. He'd made a lot of money on the side as a stripper. Even getting paid extras to sleep with members of the hen parties he showed up for. On a lot of occasions it would be the soon to be bride that wanted the extra seeing to. But he had done his fair share of mother in laws as well.

Sebastian didn't mind because in his mind it wasn't cheating. Just a cash transaction between two consenting adults. Just as long as Marco never went off with another man. That rule could never be bended or misconstrued in any way. It was set in stone for life in Sebastian's eyes.

The two men took turns in hugging Sophie tightly before sitting down on either side of her. Both not knowing what to say at first.

Zara grabbed a couple of bottles of beer from the fridge and placed them down on the coffee table in front of everyone, "think we can all do with a drink"

"If you need anything at all Sophie", Sebastian put his arm tightly around both her shoulders, "you only have to ask. Me and Marco will always be here for you. We're kind of going to be one big family some day"

Sophie sensed that he was hinting at what was suppose to happen that night between the four of them. She felt bad for letting everyone down, "I'm really sorry about tonight. I know we've been planning it for a good while. Just didn't expect something like this was gonna happen.

I know we all have to die sometime. Just doesn't make it any easier when it actually happens"

"Especially in your case", Marco blurted out, "your poor father is plastered all over the news. Can't be easy"

Sebastian gave his lover a disapproving look before turning his attention back to Sophie, "life is such a fragile thing. No one knows when they're going to go. Some live onto ninety"

"And end up shitting in a bag", Marco added.

Sebastian threw his lover another disapproving look before turning back to Sophie, "while others get snuffed out while still only a baby. Life isn't fair. The good don't always live long lives and the bad don't always suffer for their crimes. That's why heaven and hell was created to make people feel that there was something better after death, so that meant their time spent on earth could be as shite as humanly possible and that they shouldn't complain"

Sebastian was a well known atheist and loved to share his views with anyone and everyone except his highly religious family back in Nigeria. He felt that being an atheist made him a better person to work in law than most. Being held back by something that has no proof or any visible evidence, made you less able as a human being to do your job properly, and he didn't mind telling his lecturers the same thing.

Marco pulled a small see through bag from his jeans pocket. It was filled with ecstasy tablets, "pity we have no use for these tonight"

Sophie instinctively took the bag out of his hand and studied the contents. She rubbed the many colourful tablets through the thin material, as a rather unorthodox idea crossed her mind, "fuck it", she popped two of them out of the packet and swallowed them down with a quick drink of her beer.

"What are you doing?", Zara couldn't believe what she was seeing.

"I need to forget", Sophie prayed the tablets would take hold of her mind soon enough.

Marco took the tablets off Sophie and swallowed two himself, "when in Rome", he joked, before handing the tablets to Sebastian.

"You sure about this?", Zara was still unsure if this was the right thing for her fiancé.

"I'm sure", Sophie replied.

Sebastian took two tablets and handed the bag to Zara. She reluctantly took two tablets out as well and studied them in the palm of her hand. There didn't seem any point in being the odd one out that night, so she swallowed them down with a drink from her bottle. They tasted horrible as always, but the final outcome would be so worth it.

It didn't take long for the effects of the party drug to raise its energy boosting head. Time started to move faster, while conversations got more intense with each topic. Gum chewing and eye rolling behaviour led to them moving the coffee table, in the hope of creating their own miniature nightclub, with an added light from Zara's novelty disco ball, that she'd gotten for Christmas the previous year.

Sophie was loving every second of the much needed distraction. Going with the moment for all it was worth. She got more suggestible at times like this. Going with the flow of others. Made it easier not to fight when a hand led her to the bedroom. Sophie didn't pull away or say no. She so wanted a baby boy at that very moment. Hopefully in the image of her dad, and most importantly of all, Sophie was gonna call him Mattie.

Chapter Nine

Jenkins Used Motors and Van Hire was one of those businesses that most well off people would steer clear of. Gary Jenkins, the owner, had a habit of buying a lot of dodgy motors that had questionable backgrounds. For a long time he didn't need a proper base to sell from. He actually used to have a pretty good thing going by parking all his cars outside busy out of town supermarkets and sticking the prices on the windscreens of each of them.

That all went to shit when a car he had just brought a punter on a test drive in, exploded into a fiery ball of flames, just after they'd parked it back up again. The branch of Tesco's it was parked in, was not impressed one bit. They brought out a court injunction against Gary so that he couldn't use any of their car parks anymore. Soon other shopping centres around Dublin followed suit. Not because they were trying to be all fucking noble and protect the public. No, those bastards just ran to follow Tesco's because it had been made a big thing by the press.

Gary was less than impressed when a cartoon appeared of him in the tabloids, standing in front of a car showroom that was up in flames, and all that was written in the speech bubble above his head was, "FREE BUILT IN BARBECUE WITH EVERY PURCHASE", it had not been a good few months.

Thankfully there was still customers out there willing to do business with him. He'd get a lot of joyriders in who wanted to buy one of his more speedy models, but didn't want any hassle with tax, insurance or even driving licences. Gary would encourage them to show up with pretty sketchy personal identification information and the car would be there's. Then the new owners would drive the shit out of it in some empty carpark. Normally leaving it wrapped around a lamppost of some description.

Van hire was another dodgy scheme that had been quite lucrative for Gary. He'd fallen in with a rather dangerous local criminal, who went by the name Trevor Matthews. He worked for someone even more unsavoury who regularly required the use of vans for various different jobs, like transporting drugs, money and certain things that bleed, as Gary once found out when he went to clear out the back of one of his vans after Trevor had rented it for two weeks. But it was safer to ask no questions of his most loyal customer.

Unfortunately when you deal with someone so unsavoury, there's bound to be times when your vans don't come back through direct means. There had been several times when the guards had impounded them as evidence in various cases, or they'd been found burnt out along the side of some quiet country road. One time even having the body of some low level criminal in the back. Thankfully it had gotten easier for Gary to deal with such issues over time.

Gary's office was a raised prefab with poorly insulated walls that overlooked the small yard he was three months behind on the rent on. He had a shitty old computer that he barely knew how to use, sitting on a large desk that had been nicked out of a secondary school down the road. He was much more interested in flicking through his mobile phone at pictures of semi naked women on Instagram. Who needed porn when you had some twenty something dancing around in dental floss, that was trying to be passed off as a bikini.

As he scrolled down through the page of different accounts, Gary came across one belonging to Tory Summers, the best friend of his sister in law. Tory was posing in a skimpy swimsuit, while cuddling into a semi naked Heavenly Celeste.

Gary asked himself the same question that he always thought of, when he seen a provocative picture of his sister in law, "how in god's name did my brother pull a little hottie like you?"

He clicked on Tory's account and scanned through more of her semi naked photos that had Celeste in them. There was even a few were they messed kissed each other on the lips, or one would suck suggestively on the other's nipples, while staring at the camera.

There was a stirring in Gary's pants that needed to be fulfilled, so he pulled out his growing erection and sat back in his creaky office chair, while staring at the erotic images of his sister in law that moved slowly across his phone. He could imagine Celeste in that skimpy bikini, sitting on his lap as his cock pummelled in and out of her surprisingly tight fanny.

Gary liked to think that all imaginary fanny he fantasised about fucking, was tight as a virginal nun in her early twenties, and who had never ridden a horse in their life, or did gymnastics for that matter. But he highly doubted most of the women in his fantasies would actually tick that box in reality. Especially not Heavenly Celeste. Her fanny must have looked like a busted kebab with all the mickey that had been up it.

It didn't take long for Gary to shoot his load all over the undercarriage of his desk. His sticky cum dripping off the used chewing gum that had been attached underneath for many years. Gary struggled to catch his breath as he fixed his flaccid cock back carefully into his pants.

Suddenly the door of his office flew open and there stood a flustered Trevor Matthews, "hope I didn't catch you wanking again?"

"Fuck off you bastard", Gary tried to play it cool, but he knew he had been busted, "too long of a working day in this place. The tanks needed to be emptied"

"I hear that brother", Trevor had a habit of calling everyone brother. Which was strange since he actually hated his real brother, "need another van off you. Make it a shitty one that you can claim back off the insurance easily enough"

Gary stood up out of his chair and surveyed his selection of vans out through the poorly cleaned window, "take that red one over in the far corner. Just make sure you burn it out and don't leave a trace"

"Sound brother", Trevor rushed off across the yard and jumped into the red van. He then proceeded to hot wire it. Which didn't take him very long, and he was speeding out of the yard at a Garda pursuit pace.

Gary watched on in delight. He'd swapped the plates and chassis number on the old red van, for one of his newer vehicles. So hopefully his insurance company wouldn't smell a rat and pay out in full for the newer vehicle. He couldn't see it going wrong. Just as long as Trevor held up his part of the deal.

Suddenly, another dirty white battered van pulled up to the front of the yard. Gary was growing a little concerned as it was blocking the entrance. It seemed planned to some degree. But thankfully Gary's fears were soon lifted as his mother jumped out the passenger door wearing a big black fluffy fur coat that had seen better days, and probably needed a good wash. She waved to the driver as he pulled away from the kerb.

This was all Gary needed that day. A visit from his fucking mother of all people. She was most likely gonna give him shit about not wanting to go to his father's funeral. It was no business of hers what he decided to do. Unfortunately his mother never seen it that way. Didn't matter how many years had past since his father Mattie had deserted the family. Gary's mother Margaret, still considered him a member of the family.

"What can I do for the black widow on such a beautiful day?", Gary knew his mother hated that nickname, so always tried to drop it into conversation each time they met. It was like a little fuck you to the embarrassment she had become.

"Don't bloody call me that", protested Margaret, "I'm your mother for god sake and don't you go forgetting that"

"See you got a lift here", Gary rubbed the side of his mouth for effect, "and I see how you paid the guy and all"

Margaret suddenly panicked thinking that her friendly driver had left a little extra of a deposit on her face and rubbed the edge of her mouth carefully, looking for stains, only to realise that her son was taking the piss of her, "fuck off you little shit. You think very little of me"

"But am I far wrong", Gary had enough with the expected chit chat with his mother and just wanted her to get to the reason of her unexpected visit, "is this about the funeral again?"

Margaret lit up a filtered cigar and started to puff large clouds of smoke into the air, "you have to go to it. He was your dad. I know he might not have been around as much as he should have been. But your father did love the pair of you, and he found it difficult when you turned your back on him. Don't let him go in the ground without saying your goodbyes"

"We said are goodbyes years ago", Gary tried his best to contain his growing anger, "Marcus may have built bridges with dad in the past. It worked in his favour. The old man paid for all his college fees and look were he is today. Living the high life in fucking Hollywood, and married to a failed rap star. But Mattie never did anything for me"

"That's because you wouldn't fucking let him. Don't you dare forget that part. And as for your brother. I'm gonna be having words with him about getting married without even telling us. He's not too old for a clip round the ear"

"I don't blame him for not inviting us", Gary instinctively rubbed a bit of dirt off one of his car's windscreen, "the tabloids here still love to mention his name anytime I'm up in court for the smallest of fucking indiscretions. While the National Enquirer did an article on you and your black widow title. Marcus doesn't need us dragging him down any further than we already have. He's got a good career now, and a beautiful wife. I'm even surprised that he's coming back for the funeral. I know I wouldn't"

"I'm gonna tell you something that you probably won't wanna hear, but you're gonna hear it anyway", Margaret shuffled uncomfortably on the spot, "when you first set up your business here, it was struggling and it took you nearly a year to get it off the ground'

"What of it?", Gary was already fearing were her mother was going with this.

"A company named Mitchell's construction had took out a contract with you, to supply vans for their business. Who do you think was a silent partner in that company?", Margaret knew she didn't have to say anymore than that.

"For fuck sake", Gary ran his fingers through his thinning hair. He had been trying different styles of haircut to hide the problem.

Margaret put her arm around her son's broad shoulder, "you see, he did care. Mattie knew you wouldn't let him help you directly, so he figured out another way to help get your business off the ground. He was very proud of you. It's just that you never gave him the chance to let him tell you with his own words. Please come to the funeral with me and make some kind of peace with each other. He maybe dead. But that doesn't mean he isn't listening"

Gary tried not to laugh. He hated all that religious crap. He still couldn't believe that he was the product of an overly god fearing couple. Which was strange since they both didn't follow their marriage vows very well, "he's dead mam. Time for talking is over. Maybe it's for the best. I probably would have just said something that one of us would have ended up regretting. Besides, can't see you getting on too well with that Dolly one"

Margaret hated to even hear that name, "that fucking bitch. Honestly thought she had something to do with your father's death, but the guards say different. But I'm willing to ignore that bitch for the next few days, just so I can say my goodbyes to your father, and I think you should do the same. Clear the air and help aid the process of moving on with your life"

Gary was still mulling over his mother's words, when a taxi pulled up at the entrance to his yard. Out of the back climbed a young woman in ripped jeans and a baggy T-shirt. While out of the front passenger seat, stepped out Gary's little brother Marcus. Even Margaret went quiet upon seeing her youngest son.

Marcus pulled the suitcases from the booth of the taxi and the car pulled away from the kerb. He soon noticed his family watching him and gave them a little wave.

Margaret couldn't hold it together any longer and ran to Marcus for a hug, as tears rolled down her cheeks, "my little baby is home again"

Marcus was a little embarrassed, especially in front of Carla, "I missed you too mam"

Margaret soon let go of her son and started hugging Carla, "it's finally great to meet my new daughter in law"

Carla wasn't much of a hugger, but patted the old woman's back awkwardly, "nice to meet you too, but I'm not Celeste"

Margaret broke off her embrace and studied the young woman's face. She knew those Hollywood celebrities changed their faces and haircuts quiet regularly, so she hadn't questioned why Celeste had looked so different on arrival. Margaret had never met the woman in the flesh, and it seemed she never would at this rate.

"My name's Carla, Mrs Jenkins. I'm Marcus's assistant", thankfully Carla could be diplomatic when required. Which was a lot of the time in Hollywood.

"But where's Celeste?", Margaret replied, glancing at both of them in confusion.

"Me and Celeste have broke up mam", it was still hard for Marcus to say those words out loud.

"But you looked so happy in all those photos in the tabloids", Margaret had a bad habit of believing everything she read or seen from so called news outlets, "and the National Enquirer reckoned you had one of the strongest marriages in Hollywood"

"Told you before mam. Don't believe everything you read in the papers", Marcus so wanted to get off that topic, so was relieved to see his big brother approaching the small group. As usual they didn't know what to say to each other, "knew I'd find you here. No address for you anywhere online"

Gary had good reason for that. He didn't like the guards or the criminals he worked for, knowing where he lived in the city. He'd rented an apartment off an old friend and only paid in cash. The bills were all in his friend's name, so there was no paper trail back to him. It also meant that any of his sexual conquests couldn't come looking for him either, or their angry husbands. But the reason that topped all of those, was that Gary hated the thought of his mother knowing where he lived. She probably would have dropped in unannounced and never leave. It had happened before, and most likely would happen again if she got half a chance.

"You know me", Gary replied, "I like to stay under the radar as always"

"How's things with you?", Marcus found himself struggling with conversation. Something he and his brother had no problem with in the past.

"Things are ticking over nicely. Not as nicely as it is for you, but still making ends meet. So marriage wasn't for you either"

"Doesn't look that way unfortunately", Marcus could sense the sly dig in his brother's comment. He'd always told Gary in the past that he had thrown away a good thing with Aisling, and that he would live to regret his actions someday. Now it looked like that shoe was on the other foot, and no amount of him explaining how their two marriages were different, would change that.

Margaret could see her two sons were already going down a bad road and quickly intervened, "you two should stay in my house. I've got lots of room"

Gary was already doubtful, "who in god's name would give you a house?"

"Give us a lift and I'll show you"

It wasn't long until the four of them pulled up outside a semi detached house with boarded up windows and some fire damage to a poorly built extension to one side. Bags of rubbish had been dumped against the sidewall and someone had written, THE BLACK WIDOW LIVES HERE, along the battered wooden fencing along the front.

"Home sweet home", Margaret announced proudly.

"You're living here?", Marcus was horrified.

"Bet it's cheap", Carla somehow seen the positive.

"Doesn't cost me a cent. I've been squatting here for months now"

"Have you even got any power?", Gary was equally horrified, but was better at hiding it than his younger brother.

"Who needs electricity these days, when you have batteries and solar power"

"Is there solar panelling on the roof?", Marcus couldn't spot any.

"Not that type of solar lighting", Margaret felt that kind of stuff was for very rich amateurs, "no, I've got all those cheap ones you put in the garden, and I leave them outside all day and then bring them in at night. Lights the whole place up brilliantly. I get a bit of hassle off the local heroin addicts sometimes, but you can easily beat those scrawny little junkies off with easy. Isn't a slap on most of them"

"Jesus Christ mam", Gary final couldn't hide his annoyance any longer, "you can't be living under these conditions"

"Don't see you offering me a place to stay", Margaret fired back.

Gary threw his eyes up, "you know I like my privacy, but I didn't know you were living like this"

"Me and Carla where gonna stay in a hotel anyway, and you're coming with us as well mam. No way you're staying another night in this place"

"But what about my stuff?", Margaret protested.

Five minutes later, Gary and Marcus where making there way through the dark corridors of the poorly kept house. Both of them were holding a solar light that they had found in the back garden. Most of the rooms had little or no furniture in them, but there was a lot of graffiti.

Upstairs they found their mother's two suitcases filled with poorly folded clothes. There was a large mattress lying on the floor next to them, with some pillows and a duvet thrown on top. But that wasn't what caught their eye the most.

Beside the makeshift bed was an A4 sized picture frame. Inside it was a collage of photos made up of pictures of Gary, Marcus, Gary's ex wife Aisling and the grandkids. Both sons didn't have to say anything to know what the other one was thinking. They had both dropped the ball at some point, and now their mother was paying the price for their ignorance.

"I honestly didn't know she was living like this", Gary noticed the ceiling of the bedroom was bulging downwards. A clear sign that there was a bad leak in the attic.

"At least we know now. That's what's important", Marcus put the picture frame in one of the suitcases and shut them both tightly, "she can stay with me and Carla in a hotel for a few days, then we'll try and figure out something more longterm. Has to be something the local council can do"

"Have you ever seen some of the council's properties?", Gary replied, "makes this place look like the ritz"

"We'll figure it out", Marcus picked up the two suitcases and headed for the door.

Back in the car, Margaret was trying to figure out what Carla's job entailed, "do you have to get my son coffee and all that shit you see in movies?"

"It's not like that with me and Marcus", Carla felt it was best not to mention that her boss had gotten coffee more times for her than the other way round, "I do a lot of the paperwork and running around for him", more like walking, but no one else needed to know that.

"But he is doing well for himself?", Margaret asked. She had read the gossip columns from America, and wasn't sure whether to believe a lot of the stuff they were saying about the financial viability of her son's films. They'd been getting great reviews, but not pulling in the cinema goers, or pay to view streaming viewers of late.

"He's doing fine Mrs Jenkins, don't you be worrying about that", Carla felt it was better to lie. The poor woman had enough worries in her life right now. She didn't need anymore bullshit to murky the waters any further.

"That's great to hear", Margaret let out a deep breath that she didn't even know she was holding in, "wait till you have kids of your own. You always think that they're going to be less of a worry when they hit eighteen and become an adult. But it actually gets so much worse. You don't know where they are all the time and you can't really help them fight their battles anymore"

"Must of been hard bringing them up on your own", Carla felt that Margaret should at least hear one of her crowning achievements coming from someone else's mouth.

"It was tougher for them to see less of their father", Margaret got lost in her own thoughts for a few moments, "it was tough for me as well. It was just that I couldn't show it to anyone. Had to stay strong for the kids. Couldn't let my neighbours or my ex in laws see how much I was hurting. The amount of times I cried myself to sleep at night. Wouldn't wash my bedsheets for months because I wanted that feeling of Mattie still beside me in the bed. Took me a long time before I started trying to get over him. Bringing men home from the pub for one night stands. Letting them climb on top of me and closing my eyes and they pushed themselves deep inside me. Then for the next half hour to an hour, I'd pretend it was my Mattie inside me. Tears came to my eyes many a night back then. Might have been a good thing really because it scared off most of the fellas after they got their bit.

"It's always a positive when you don't have to wake up the next morning beside the fuckers", Carla joked.

"Ain't that the fucking truth", Margaret wiped a tear from her eye, before noticing her two sons returning to the car with her belongings, "my two precious men are back"

Marcus loaded the cases into the booth, as Gary got back in the driver's seat and turned on the engine, "Jesus mam, why the fuck didn't you tell me that you where staying in a dive like that?"

"I didn't want you worrying son", Margaret replied.

Marcus got back in the car and put on his seatbelt, "that's us sorted. He looked in the rear view mirror and caught the eyes of his mother, "now mam. Tell us where you'd like to stay in Dublin and your wish is my command?"

"The Gresham", Margaret announced proudly. She'd always had a thing for the place, ever since that elderly American tourist had brought her back to his suite for champagne and caviar. A totally disgusting drinking snack, but still sounded good to boast to others about.

"Then the Gresham it is", Marcus was delighted to put a smile on his mother's face once more. Just a pity it couldn't stay there over the next few days.

Chapter Ten

"What do you think is in the coffin?", Rory asked as he shuffled uncomfortably on the spot. He was regretting wearing his work clothes to the funeral home, for the viewing of Mattie Jenkins body. Unfortunately it turned out that no one was allowed to view the body. Supposedly there wasn't that many recognisable parts left to say that was definitely a lump of Mattie.

"I suppose they just bucketed up what they could find, and placed it inside", Bernard was shocked by how expensive the coffin looked. It had holy figures carved into every area of the timber. But one of them was troubling him more than others, "do you think that character in the middle looks like a Jedi?"

"Like a fucking what?", Rory whispered.

"Like a Star Wars Jedi", Bernard was adamant that he was right, "if you look at it carefully, you can see the long cloak, and he even looks like he's holding a lightsaber. If I had to go out on a limb here, I'd even say he looks like that character that Liam Neeson played. You know, in the shit one"

Rory tilted his head slightly to one side, "it does a bit"

"They shouldn't be burying him like this", muttered a zombie like old man in a suit, who sat on one of the chairs that had been lined up at one end of the large mahogany covered walled room.

"What's that mate?", Bernard asked.

"They couldn't find all of Mattie", the suited old man didn't look up from the floor, "I tried searching for the rest of his body, but there was too much area to cover and we were losing the light. I'd say animals got the rest of him"

Rory couldn't stop thinking about what state his friend's body was in, "what part of him could they not find?"

"His head", the old man moaned, "you can't be really buried if you don't have your head with you. It's the main part of your body. Helps you think, speak, hear, talk and many many more wonderfully things that makes life so special"

"Licking some fine fanny out", Bernard whispered to Rory, who nodded in agreement.

A young blonde dressed all in black, came out from a door that was marked, STAFF ONLY, and knelt down beside the sobbing old man, "you need to calm down Mr Cruise and take a few deep breaths. You did your best for your friend Mattie and you shouldn't be knocking yourself up so much over his death. It wasn't your fault"

Spencer Cruise hugged the young woman tightly, "I know I shouldn't Katie. It's just difficult to see my friend being buried without all his parts. It's just not right"

"I know it's not, but you did your best to make sure that wouldn't happen. Unfortunately life's not always fair", Katie was good at dealing with the grieving customers who unwantingly frequented her father's funeral home. She could connect with them on a level that few could.

"Better to bury half of something, than none of anything", that had sounded better in Bernard's head before he had said it out loud.

There was an awkward silence before Katie turned her attention back to Spencer, "maybe you should go home and get some rest. Sitting here all day won't make those negative thoughts go away that are haunting your mind. You need a distraction from all this"

Spencer stood up out of his chair as an idea flashed across his mind, "you're right. I need to be doing something with my time that will benefit my dear friend in someway"

"That's it. Something that will help you deal with the grieving process", Katie felt her words were hitting home. That always gave her a warm feeling inside.

"I'm gonna go back out to the canal and find Mattie's head", Spencer proudly announced to the few people in the room.

"That's not what I meant", Katie quickly tried to backtrack on her words.

But Spencer wasn't listening as he marched off towards the exit with a new spring in his step.

Rory had been listening to everything going on in the room, but his eyes had been drawn mostly to the two beautiful legs that Katie had on show in her tight skirt, that stopped a good few inches above the knee. Not something he was expecting a funeral home worker to be wearing. Normally it was men who did this part of the job, not a hot young blonde with a figure that most other women would kill for. Rory was already trying to figure out ways of being charming and what suitable chat up line he could use under the circumstances. But unfortunately recent knock backs were still playing on his mind. What if this young attractive blonde just seen him as another fragile old man like that red head of recent weeks. He wasn't sure could his ego take it.

"The poor guy seems distraught", Rory was trying his best to think of a good opening line that would fit in well with his surroundings, and that seemed it.

"He was there when it happened", Katie replied.

"You mean he seen Mattie being turned into purée?", Bernard wasn't one to think out his sentences before speaking.

Rory threw his friend a dirty look, before turning his attentions back to an already shocked Katie, "please don't mind my friend. He's grieving in his own obscure way"

Katie was used to all manner of different types of mourning among the many people who had frequented her family's funeral home since she first got to help out behind the scenes at the tender age of fourteen. By fifteen she was embalming bodies on her own, and by eighteen she was in charge of whole funeral services. Katie wasn't squeamish in any way. But the only thing that did shock her from time to time was the attitude of some of the mourners. That's if you could really call some of them that. Some people just showed up for a good nosey and see who else was there. There was also these other types that had this twisted interest in going to funerals that had nothing to do with them. The more gruesome or heartbreaking, the better. They just seemed to feed off the negative emotions in the church. Like a new sponge touching water for the first time. It was sickening to watch such behaviour, but Katie had no way of stopping it. Unless the family said otherwise, all was welcome to the day of the funeral, even the bad.

"That's okay", Katie spotted the type of mourner Bernard was from the very start. He was the old sleazy guy who would probably use someone's grief to get their knickers off later that night. Unfortunately it wasn't that rare from what Katie had noticed in the past, and had trained herself to ignore the activities of the predators, as she liked to call them, at funerals she overseen, "it's just that Mr Cruise has been struggling a lot since that faithful day. Blames himself for Mattie's death"

"Why's that?", Rory was already lost in the young woman's beautiful green eyes.

"They had flipped a coin for the spot, and Mr Cruise had called it", Katie rubbed her fingers along the smooth grooves in Mattie's coffin, "amazing how life can all boil down to the flip of a coin"

"Ain't that the fucking truth", Bernard unfortunately added, "I once had to flip a coin with this asshole here", he playfully punched Rory in the shoulder, "over who was getting the hot twenty eight year old and who had to shag her minger friend. I got the fucking friend, so I know where poor Mr Cruise is coming from"

"I'm sure you do", Katie was already planning on giving Bernard a wide berth for the rest of her time dealing with Mattie's funeral.

Outside in the small carpark, Ellis was sitting along in her car, crying. Her boyfriend Steven had refused to come with her to see her father's body. Well, more just the coffin, since no one was allowed to look at what was left of her father inside that overpriced neatly carved wooden box.

Ellis would have much preferred to see her father cremated in a private ceremony with just the family and closest friends, but her mother had been adamant that the event had to be big and bold. Even hiring legendary Irish country star, the Mushy Pea.

That might have been a good idea thirty years ago, but the Mushy Pea was now a total burned out alcoholic that normally ended up verbally abusing his audience, or trying to hit on any woman with a pulse. He could either show up and make the day totally unique and special, or he could ruin it all with another one of his tantrums. Only time would tell.

Three parked vehicles down from Ellis, was another car occupied by Gary, Marcus, Margaret and Carla. They had been running a bit late thanks to Margaret falling asleep in the giant jacuzzi bath that was in her hotel room. She'd also learnt the joys of room service and had already worked up a rather large hefty bill for her son to pay. Mostly made up with bottles of champagne and garlic bread starters. Her breath now smelling like the air vent at an overworked pizzeria.

They all piled out of Gary's car and Margaret lit up a cigarette before anyone had a chance to tell her that they were in a hurry to get inside.

Margaret looked over at the large featureless building that contained the body of her ex husband, "to think we'll all end up in here someday. I'd much rather be burned like one of those Viking ceremonies. Pushed out on a small fishing boat into the Liffey, and my friends watch on as it burns down to the waterline. Now that would be a way to go"

"Don't think Dublin County Council would allow that mam", Marcus was used to outlandish requests off people in Hollywood, so his mother's ideas didn't seem that over the top.

"I put it in my will that I want free wifi installed on my gravestone", Carla suddenly announced.

"Why would you want that?", asked a shocked Marcus.

"Because then there'll be all these teenagers hanging around my grave all the time, and passerby's will think I once was very important or influential in some way", Carla had put a surprising amount of thought into this and nothing was gonna change her mind.

It was then that Gary noticed Ellis crying in her car. He walked over and gently opened the car door. At first she got a bit of a shock, but that soon turned to relief as she jumped out of the driver's seat and hugged her older brother tightly around his waist. Burying her teary eyes into his chest and sobbing loudly.

"It's okay Ellis", Gary still felt weird trying to console a young woman who he had only really gotten to know recently. Their brother, sister bond still growing over that time.

"I miss him so much", Ellis fired out a load more of fresh tears.

"I know you do", Gary patted her back gently. He so wanted to say something that would put his half sister's mind at easy, but he just wasn't feeling the same emotions as she was now dealing with and probably never would.

Margaret watched on as her eldest son comforted a member of what she liked to call, the enemy Jenkins family, "didn't know Gary was getting on with that lot now"

Marcus was surprised as well. Not because he felt any ill will against his half sisters. It was more to do with the fact that it was so out of character for his brother to be so compassionate. He'd become pretty much a hard hearted middle aged man over time, "maybe he's softening up with age"

"I highly doubt that", Margaret replied.

Suddenly Aisling appeared out of nowhere and gave Margaret a big hug, "so nice to see you again. Must be years now"

Margaret was delighted to see Aisling as well and hugged her tightly, "I missed you too"

The pair started to chatter on as if no one else was around.

Carla nudged Marcus discreetly, "who's the little hottie hugging your mother?"

"She's my ex sister in law", Marcus hated to agree with Carla, but Aisling was definitely a hottie. She may have been a good bit older since he'd last seen her, but Aisling had actually gotten better looking in that time. And her wonderful personality had always been a breath of fresh air during even the worst family crises they had to deal with over the years. Marcus had always resented his brother for having such a wonderful woman in his life, and hated him even more when he treated her like shite by fucking all those other women that couldn't hold a candle to Aisling's beauty.

Margaret finally broke off her embrace and did the introductions, "I'm sure you remember Marcus"

Aisling instinctively hugged him tightly into her perky bosoms, "I'm so sorry about your father. I know you were all distant with him in recent years, but he was still a good man deep down"

Marcus was trying his hardest not to get an erection. It had always been an embarrassing habit of his to grow a mini chubby, anytime he was in close proximity to Aisling. Anything could set him off. The smell of her perfume. A toss of her long dark hair. A bit of bare flesh on show. The worst being at his brother's wedding when he'd asked her out to dance near the end of the night and she graciously accepted. Marcus had been drinking since earlier that day and was feeling a little more at ease than normal. Aisling had pulled him close on the dance floor. Their bodies both sweating from all the dancing that night. Then it happened. His purple headed warrior stood to attention like a uniformed guard in front of the queen. There was no half mast with this fella. He just shot up like a Jack in the box. Aisling had thankfully not recoiled in horror that night. She just danced with Marcus while all the time asking him to try and lower his mast. After a few tense minutes it finally went down. The song ended and Aisling smiled and said her goodbyes. It was never talked about since that night. At first Marcus had thought it was for the best. But over time he felt it had been a wasted opportunity to tell Aisling how he felt about her. Unfortunately an erection doesn't say I love you, half as much as the real words could.

"And this is Carla, Marcus's assistant", Margaret announced proudly, in the hope some other people in the area could hear her words.

Aisling went in for a handshake, but Carla was already vying for a hug instead. Embracing the attractive woman tightly in her small arms.

It didn't take long for Marcus to realise that his assistant was hoping to fuck the woman he still had a big crush on. This had to be the images and emotions that nightmares were built on.

Gary brought over Ellis to meet the rest of his family. Introductions were a bit stand offish at first, but of course Aisling was in with the big hugs again and embraced Ellis tightly, "it's so nice to finally meet you"

"And you", Ellis replied, quickly feeling a little stupid since she hadn't a clue who this woman even was.

Margaret glanced at her watch, "think we should get inside before the larger crowds start arriving for prayers. Can't stand all that holy stuff"

The group started to move towards the door of the building, but Marcus grabbed Carla's arm and pulled her back, "please don't tell me you're gonna try and fuck my ex sister in law"

"What if I am?", Carla replied with a big smile, "Aisling's hot and not with your brother anymore, so she's fair game in my opinion"

Marcus was struggling to word his reasons why, without wearing his heart on his sleeve, "but she's married with kids to some new fella"

"But if she wants to wander a little, why can't I be the one to guide her to the dark side?"

"Because it doesn't seem right"

"Sounds more like it doesn't sound right to you and you alone"

"You don't even know if she's into women", Marcus protested.

"Either do you", then it dawned on Carla, "you fancy her, don't you?"

Marcus realised his heart had been ripped out and placed on display for all to see, but he wasn't going to admit it that freely, "I don't know what you mean"

"I don't know what you mean", Carla mockingly copied Marcus's high pitch tone, before dropping back to her normal voice, "you know exactly what I mean. You've got a thing for your ex sister in law and you're afraid of anyone else going there except you. Am I right?"

"You're right", Marcus threw his eyes up in despair.

"Are you gonna even tell her how you feel?"

"Doesn't seem like the right time"

"When is", Carla pulled out her blackjack flavoured vape and took a quick hit, "I met my longest ever girlfriend at my granny's funeral. Grief brings strong emotions out of people. Don't let this day slide without having a word in her ear. If you don't, I will", and with that, Carla marched after the rest of their group, leaving Marcus to wallow in his own growing regrets.

Back inside the funeral home, Rory was still trying to charm the young blonde. He was now regretting that he hadn't made an effort with his choice of clothing. He smelt of wet plaster board and paint thinners.

"Will you be personally dealing with the Jenkins family over the next few days?", Rory literally had his fingers crossed behind his back.

"All the way to the grave", it was a line that Katie had gotten used to using with all people besides the direct family of her many unwilling customers. Sounded too much like an insensitive company slogan.

"So what do you do with your spare time?", Rory was already looking for an opening.

"This takes up most of my time", Katie replied.

"But you must get time off, and I doubt you spend it sitting at home planning your next busy day at the funeral home"

"No", Katie flashed a perfect smile his way. She could see were this was going and was happy to play along for now, "I go the gym and enjoy the odd live concert here and there", she looked Rory up and down. Taking in the dirt of his clothing, "you look like a busy man yourself. Do you get much time to enjoy the finer things in life yourself?"

"Don't let the clothes fool you young lady", Bernard busted into their conversation like an unwanted snot in a fruit salad, "we both run our own building businesses. And we prefer to be hands on", he attempted to mime his hands on approach, but ended up looking like he was groping some invisible woman's perky breasts.

"I bet you do", Katie was start to get a strong sense of sleaze off Bernard.

Bernard tapped the side of the coffin, "go on and tell us what's inside?. Bet it's a load of see through bags filled with entrails and jagged strips of human flesh"

"For fuck sake Bernard", Rory threw his eyes up in despair, "you don't ask shit like that. Especially not in the bloody funeral home when the family are about to walk in", he gestured towards the open doorway for effect.

Unfortunately Rory was a tad too on the money and there in the doorway stood Margaret, her sons, Aisling, Carla and a weeping Ellis. They all looked pretty shocked, and most likely heard Bernard's question.

But Bernard wasn't put off in anyway and just waved over at them all, "hi folks. Thought you would have been here earlier. Me and Rory are just getting to know your one here. She's running the show over the next few days"

It wasn't long until they had all made their introductions. Some new and some just catching up after many years. They'd all at some point ran their fingers along the coffin lid. Each one wondering the very same thing. What did poor old Mattie Jenkins look like inside?. Of course the tabloids had not helped with the mental images for the family, as they had printed stories about how the poor man's body was obliterated by the shell, that nobody still seemed to know how it ended up in a quiet canal in the middle of Meath. That seemed to be a question that would never be answered.

Many mourners had arrived over the next half hour. A lot of them Margaret and her sons had no knowledge of. Most likely they had come along after the original Jenkins family had been tossed to the sidelines. It hurt Margaret to see how much their lives had divided. Mattie had gone from strength to strength without her. That was a bitter pill to swallow.

Gary still had Ellis hugging into him when a familiar face stepped in the door. It was his old friend Lucas. They'd hung around with each other from childhood, all the way up until eighteen, when Lucas had gone onto college in Belfast, and they had never seen each other again.

But the years had been kinder to Lucas. He may have been in his forties, but the guy had definitely looked after himself. His hair was dyed and his skin looked perfect tanned as always. Probably thanks to his Spanish mother, who Gary had wanked off to, hundreds of times. Hard to get the image of a sunbathing topless woman out of your mind, when you're only thirteen.

Margaret was the first to welcome her son's old friend, who at one point she seen like another son. She was up off her chair and threw her arms around Lucas, enveloping him in her thick furry coat, "I'm so glad you came Lucas. Mattie used to think so much of you"

"Couldn't believe it when I seen the papers", Lucas spoke with a mild feminine accent. Something he had been badly bullied in school for, along with his slightly camp personality.

"The papers just like to stick the knife in and keep twisting", Margaret had robbed a fair few stacks of tabloids from outside several newsagents. That was until Rory had pointed out that there was no real point in doing that, since most of the news was online these days.

Gary would have preferred not to open dialogue with his old friend again. He had spent so long trying to move on and forget their past, that speaking now would have seemed counterproductive. But he had no choice and apologised to Ellis as he slipped out from her reach. Thankfully Aisling took over consoling the young woman.

Margaret was still hugging Lucas when Gary had made himself known, "long time no see", he had tried to play it cool, but straight away his nerves were getting to him. Gary couldn't understand why. Over twenty five years had past between them. Those confusing few years were in the past now. They were both mature men these days and should be able to act accordingly. So why was there a trickle of sweat running down the centre of Gary's back?.

Margaret thumped her son's shoulder hard, "is that all you can say to your best friend?"

"In his defence": Lucas calmly spoke, "we haven't seen each other in a very long time"

Margaret looked her son up and down suspiciously, "bet that was his fault and all"

"It was both our faults", Lucas replied, "we just drifted apart like most people", he turned to Gary, "isn't that about right?"

"It is unfortunately", Gary was thankfully for the save from his old friend.

Margaret seemed happy with their answers, "okay then. I'll leave you two to talk", she then pointed at Lucas, "and don't you be such a stranger in future"

"I definitely won't", Lucas replied.

Margaret then went back to her seat and left the two old friends to talk in private.

"How did you hear about my dad?", Gary asked without thinking.

"Kind of hard to miss it with all the news coverage", Lucas replied, trying his best not to break a smile.

"Oh right", Gary felt a little stupid and quickly tried to move things along, "I'm glad that you're here"

"No way could I let your father be buried without paying my final respects. He was always good to me growing up. Way better than my own father ever was. Remember the time I was getting chased by that gang, and he was driving past. He stopped the car and threatened to dig the heads of them, if they didn't leave me alone?"

"Pity they didn't listen", Gary smirked, "they ended up smashing his back window in"

"But he did save me from a pretty bad beating that day, and I'll always remember him for that", Lucas glanced over at the closed coffin, "just a pity that I can't say my goodbyes properly. Not a nice way to go"

"That it wasn't", Gary wished he had fond memories of his father like most other people in attendance that day, but unfortunately the negatives kept bubbling to the surface and covering all else that was trying to bust through from below. It was gonna be a tough few days of feigning emotions that he was far from feeling himself.

Chapter Eleven

"Mam, we are already late", Sophie protested, "why in god's name would you agree to collect Cilla and Frank?"

Cilla being Sophie's auntie. Named after the famous Liverpool singer, and strangely enough, actually had a decent singing voice that was starting to weaken in recent years. Cilla had married a man called Frank Black. Most people felt she only did this because of his surname, and that she wanted to further her musical career. But that couldn't be further from the truth.

Poor Frank had a rather serious accident when he was a young man, that had left him partially sighted. He'd gotten a rather hefty payout at the time and was living the high life. Cilla wanted to be permanently part of that, so she had agreed to marry him.

Unfortunately the money ran out and Frank ended up blind from the irreparable damage to his eyes. Cilla began singing in pubs and restaurants, while Frank became a bit of a well known perv with his constant wandering hands, that mostly found there way onto the bodies of the younger women in the family. Whenever anyone got annoyed with Frank's behaviour, he'd just cry and complain about how he was still getting used to his condition, thirteen years after being officially declared blind.

"I need my sister by my side", protested Dolly as she checked her makeup in the provided mirror in the back of the stretched limo that she had booked for today and tomorrow, "speaking of sisters, where the hell is Ellis?. Can't get a hold of her on the phone all morning"

Ellis went ahead in her own car", Sophie so wished her sister had of come with them in the limo. At least then she wouldn't have to deal with her mother all on her own.

"Don't worry Mrs Jenkins", Zara was trying her best to help, but was failing badly, "Ellis will be there when we arrive. Just try and relax and breathe a few deep breaths", Zara tried to simulate the intaking and out taking of air with her hands.

"I don't need air", Dolly protested, "I need a drink, and more importantly I need my husband back", the pain and hurt she was feeling, flashed across her face, but Dolly buried it back under the layers of makeup, just as quickly.

The limo door opened and Frank was ushered inside with his walking stick. He was in his early seventies and wore a pair of thick shades. Didn't help that he insisted on wearing a jet black shaggy wig that gave him the look of Roy Orbison. Well, a long dead Roy Orbison that someone had recently dug up from his resting place and dusted off the cobwebs and hungry maggots.

Frank was sat down next to Zara and Cilla pushed in beside him, fixing her dyed red hair as she tried to look a little less unflustered.

Cilla did her best not to show her age. She was twelve years older than her sister and definitely looked every bit of it. The years hadn't been kind to her and neither had the bottle of whiskey a day habit she had as well. A functioning alcoholic at its finest.

"Sorry about the delay", Cilla muttered as she searched her oversized handbag for her trusty mouth spray, "took long enough to get this pain in the arse out of bed and dressed", she elbowed her husband roughly in the shoulder, "you wouldn't believe the amount of times I wished this morning, that it was this old fool that had of gotten blown up by that shell"

"For god sake Cilla", Sophie protested. She was used to her auntie's toxic tongue, but still never made it any less hurtful when Cilla went in with all guns blazing, which wasn't even one of those times.

"Look sis", Dolly was quick to intervene, "this day is stressful enough and I haven't the head for any more hassle, so please keep stuff like that to yourself"

Before Cilla had a chance to answer, the uncomfortable silence was suddenly broken by Zara protesting at Frank's withered hand wandering onto her chunky thigh once again, "get it off old man or I'll break it the fuck off"

"Sorry love", Frank loosened his grip off Zara's thigh, before patting her leg gently, "thought you were the armrest"

"I highly doubt that", Zara got up in the cramped interior and moved over beside Sophie and Dolly.

Cilla linked her fingers with her husband's, "my poor Frank is still struggling with his lack of sight, Zara. If you're gonna be in this family longterm, you'll have to get use to these little mistakes", she turned to her husband and fixed his already neat tie, "isn't that right love?"

"That's absolutely correct my dear", a sleazy smile filled Frank's face. It wasn't directed at anyone in particular, but Sophie and Zara knew it was for them.

Frank had recently taken a keen interest in Sophie and Ellis. When they had turned eighteen he had started to describe them as legal tender, and like all good banknotes, they needed to be caressed regularly to check the quality, and boy did that dirty old bastard caress them. Then when Frank found out about Sophie's relationship with Zara. He made sure to make an appearance at any family event after that. Always going in for long lingering hugs with added firm rubs of the back. People had always advised the girls that you had to be more compassionate and patient with someone blind, but the same bloody people probably never had to deal with a sleazy old pervert like Frank.

A good part of the journey was completed in silence, with some minor whispering between different groups in the back of the limo.

That was until Cilla bridged the gap once more, "what if Mattie's old family is at the funeral home. What are you going to do?"

"I haven't the head for Margaret today ", Dolly had been keeping her concerns to herself.

It had been easy in the early days to shape Mattie into the perfect husband and dashing older man to bring to dinner parties, were they met all the right people to be seen with. Unfortunately Margaret and her kids were like a millstone around their necks. Dolly had tried to be civil at first and told Mattie that he had to have some connection with his two sons. But the fighting between Mattie and Margaret had gotten worse over time and soon the weekly visits to his old family home had became unbearable. He'd pulled away from his two sons for the good of everyone.

"Just tell her to fuck off", Cilla suggested, "or let me go into the funeral home first and talk to the staff. I can tell them that Margaret and her cronies have no right to be there and that there should be bouncers positioned at all entrances to make sure that none of their lot get into see Mattie"

"Don't think you can do that with a funeral", Zara had learnt over her time in the family, that it was better to stay out of most family discussions, but as like most of them, this one was cruising into the absurd once again. Dolly and Cilla had a habit of thinking the world revolved around them. That might have worked in some ways for Dolly with her money and power, but Cilla had neither, but still insisted on acting the same way. Riding on the coattails of her younger sister.

"We can do what we like", Cilla hated to be contradicted by anyone. But especially by someone who she considered inferior.

Unfortunately Cilla had never grown to embrace the multicultural place that Ireland had become in recent decades, and still seen anyone that hadn't got white skin as either an asylum seeker, restaurant staff or hospital worker. She just couldn't grasp the fact that everyone was on a level playing field these days, and she had no interest in learning that either.

"Look, we'll just show up and see what's happening", Dolly didn't need civil unrest in her own camp, "play it by ear. Maybe none of that lot have bothered showing up. Been a long time since any of them have seen Mattie. People have a tendency to have short memories and move on just as quickly. I'm sure it will be okay"

Sophie rubbed her mother's arm, "it'll be fine mam. Don't be worrying"

Fifteen minutes later, they pulled into the carpark of the funeral home, that was now filled with Hi-Ace vans and a few newly bought cars that most likely belonged to friends of Dolly. But the vans were an eyesore. Parked poorly all around the place, even outside the gates on the footpath. There wasn't even enough room for the limo driver to pull the whole way into the carpark, so he just left the back of his vehicle hanging out onto the road.

Sophie climbed out of the back, before helping her mother out. Then Zara followed, trying to pretend she didn't feel Frank's (helping) hand on her ass. She said nothing and just gave herself a good distance from the dirty old bastard when he finally got out as well.

"I can't believe this shit", Dolly couldn't take her eyes off all the battered dirty vans that surrounded her. It was like a traveller camp had set up home in the carpark.

But Sophie had other concerns on her mind, "Is that singing I can hear?"

Everyone went quiet in the group, as they all strained their ears to hear. Yes indeed, there was singing coming from inside the funeral home. Not beautiful hymns or haunting Enya songs, but it sounded more like a drunken singsong at the end of a long day in the pub.

When they approached the main entrance, there was a number of older men standing outside in their work clothes. There was also a strong smell of marijuana hanging in the air. Dolly barged through them all and arrived at the reception desk that must have only been recently put in, because the pine material it was made from, still looked fresh.

The owner of the funeral home, Mr Wilson, was standing behind the counter with a very nervous look on his face, which broke into a cold sweat when he seen Dolly coming through the door. He wiped the sweat from his brow and tried to act like everything was okay, "good afternoon Mrs Jenkins. I'm so sorry about your husband. He was a good man"

"Less of your bullshit and start explaining why this place is looking like a country pub on a Friday afternoon?", Dolly plonked her large handbag down on the counter and took out her vape for a quick hit.

"Sorry but you can't vape in here", announced the middle aged receptionist.

"You've got fellas smoking hash outside those doors, and you're giving me shit about a vape!. For god sake"

"Please calm down mam", Sophie rubbed her mother's arm again.

"I can't calm down", Dolly protested, "I want this lot gone"

"People come from all over to pay their respects", Mr Wilson tried his best to put a better spin on things, "from my personal experience, when you get a lot of people in the same room, and they haven't seen each other in years, sometimes it can get a bit raucous"

"There's raucous Mr Wilson and then there's a god damn travesty like what's going on here", Dolly tried to fix her few stray blonde hairs back into place and get a bit of dignity back in her appearance, "and if you are not willing to deal with this situation, then I shall", and with that, she stormed off down the long corridor towards the noisy singing.

Dolly stormed in the door and took no prisoners, "right then, everyone out, you disrespectful lot of inbred bastards"

Sophie tapped her mother on the shoulder, "wrong room mam"

Dolly hadn't been paying much attention to who was in the room and finally focused her eyes on the few priests and nuns that sat around a cheap wooden coffin that contained the body of an elderly nun. Dolly tried her best to edge out of the room discreetly without saying too much else, except, "sorry about that, wrong room"

When Dolly had finally found the right room, she struggled to get inside, as there was many people leaning against the door on the other side. Thankfully Zara used her body weight to push the door open, and the small group stepped into a room full of poorly dressed people singing king of the road. Which was Mattie's favourite song.

Margaret was sitting amongst the noisy group, laughing and joking with the men. But that's not what pissed off Dolly the most, because sitting two down from Margaret, was her own daughter Ellis, singing along with the rest of them and laughing. This was a betrayal of the highest order, and Dolly wasn't going to take it lying down.

"I want everyone out now", shouted Dolly, but unfortunately her idea of a shout these days wasn't what you would call loud.

Nobody reacted as they all started into another chorus of king of the road.

"Sophie nudged Zara, "please can you tell them to stop?. They'll hear your voice over the singing"

Zara didn't need much encouragement and let rip, "SHUT THE FUCK UP THE LOT OF YOUSE"

The singing quickly stopped and an awkward silence filled the room. Margaret and Dolly's eyes met, and a mutual hatred filled both their thoughts. Dolly couldn't remember the last time she'd come face to face with her husband's ex wife, but it wasn't long enough in her opinion.

"I just knew you were gonna show up sooner or later and ruin all the fun", Margaret gestured to the people around her, "me and Mattie's old friends here, were just trying to honour him with a few verses from his favourite song.

But you always hated Mattie's past and the people who were in it"

"I want you and your scummy family out of here now, and bring this horde of degenerates with you", Margaret was aware that she was well in the minority, but she was known to rarely back down in an argument.

"I'm no fucking degenerate", Gary jumped up from his seat, as if that one word was the worst insult he had ever heard in his life. Which it wasn't. Didn't even come close.

Ellis put herself between her mother and Gary, "why do you have to be such a totally bitch mam. These people are here to say goodbye to my dad. They all think so much of him, and you want to drive them away", she then gestured towards Gary and Marcus, "and they are my brothers. Never got to be a part of their lives, because you wouldn't allow it"

"It was for the best", Margaret poorly pleaded as she still tried to look ready for anything that might come her way in the next few minutes.

"The best for who?", Sophie replied, "not me anyway, and definitely not Sophie"

Sophie really didn't wanna be dragged into this mess, but felt she had no choice at this point, "mam had her reasons"

Cilla pushed Frank towards an unwanting Zara to mind, and strode forward, "I've enough of this shit. All of you fucking out now, or I'll call the guards"

"Fuck this shit", Margaret had enough, "we're going", she then turned to the rest of the people in the large room, "WHO'S COMING BACK TO MURPHY'S PUB FOR A DRINKING SESSION IN HONOUR OF MATTIE?"

The whole crowd cheered and started to swarm out of the room through a fire exit door in the corner.

Margaret's entourage started to follow, but she waited until last, to get one final say in against her replacement, "you may have took my husband from me, but you never fully took his heart. We both know that", she then marched proudly out the door.

Gary was standing at the door and looked back into the room, "you coming Ellis?"

Ellis went to leave, but her mother grabbed her arm, "you can't go off with that lot"

"Why not?", Ellis protested.

"Because we're your family", Cilla made it sound more like a threat than anything.

"Gary and Marcus are my family as well", and with that, Ellis pulled her arm free from her mother's grip and stormed out of the room.

Rory and Bernard was still watching on amused at what just happened. Both of them leaning on Mattie's coffin as if it was a makeshift bar. All they were short was the pints of beer. Katie had discreetly hid behind a pillar when it all kicked off. Last thing she wanted was to play referee between warring families.

"You wanna come the pub with me and Bernard?", Rory asked the young woman.

Katie stepped out from the shadows and caught the nasty glares from Dolly and her sister. She tried her best to ignore it, "I better not. Looks like I have my work cut out for me here"

Bernard was already heading for the exit, "you heard the lady, she's busy with work. Now get your ass moving", he smiled over at Dolly and her family, "maybe a couple of you fine ladies might like to join us?"

Frank glanced around the room, as if his blindness had suddenly been cured, "what fine ladies is that fella on about?"

"He's on about us", Cilla quickly scolded.

Rory was still disappointed that he couldn't convince Katie to join them, but he still gave it would last attempt to build some kind of bond with the younger woman, "maybe I'll see you tomorrow at the funeral?"

"You most definitely shall", Katie joked back.

Rory made his escape out the exit door, leaving poor Katie alone to explain to the rest of Mattie's family, why the funeral home had turned into an impromptu party. This wasn't gonna be easy.

Chapter Twelve

"I'm staying out here as long as it takes, to find the rest of Mattie", Spencer announced proudly down the phone to his wife Michelle. He could of just said head, but that didn't sound right, and a bit disrespectful.

"Does that mean you won't be home tonight?", asked a strangely eager Michelle.

"There's a strong chance that I might be out here until morning, but don't be waiting up worrying. I know this area pretty well", Spencer lied. He hadn't been there that many times and normally he'd just stick by the canal or nearby river.

"Well you don't be worrying about me. I'm going out with Alfonso tonight for a few drinks", Alfonso was this new friend of Michelle who she kept telling Spencer was gay, but that never seemed to stop Alfonso from playfully grabbing her ass all the time.

Spencer had hoped to bridge this complaint with his wife a few days ago, but unfortunately a last minute spa experience package became available, so Michelle and Alfonso had gone off into town and booked a hotel room for the night, with the excuse that, "you wouldn't want me driving home after a day of bottomless Prosecco?"

Spencer had his comeback on the tip of his tongue. That they could of gotten the Dart into town and back. A fifteen minute journey in total. But he hadn't the head or heart to fight with his beautiful wife any longer. Spencer knew he was losing her. He just didn't know how to win her around. How could he possibly compete with the men she had been seen in the company of.

"Okay dear. Enjoy yourself", these cheerful replies were getting harder to fake with each week, "love you", he waited for those words to be said back to him, but they never came.

"Talk to you tomorrow", and with that, Michelle ended the call.

Spencer sat down on the edge of his open car booth and contemplated what the future might have in store for his marriage. It was sinking into the icy depths, faster than the Titanic. There was no way of saving it.

Then a peculiar thought crossed Spencer's mind. What if, by finding Mattie's head, that suddenly his wife would see him as a hero. People would be cheering his impossible achievement. If others thought he was great, then maybe Michelle would too.

Spencer pulled on his waterproof dungarees and wellies, before locking up his car for the night. The area was pretty quiet, but there was still a strong chance that it could be vandalised or robbed while he was gone. It was a busy carpark during the day, but at night it turned into a quiet place for drug heads to get high in their cars.

Spencer hadn't time to be worrying about such things. He put on his backpack and marched off into the wilderness in search of his friend's head.

Chapter Thirteen

Murphy's pub was packed that night with a mixture of
Mattie's friends and local drinkers. But they'd all kind of
mixed together in one big glorious drinking party. There
had been a professional karaoke machine booked for that
night, and it had now turned into an impromptu singing
tribute to Mattie. Family and friends were singing songs
that he either loved or reminded people of him.

Mattie had been a big fan of the Proclaimers, so a
slightly tipsy Marcus had decided to sing letter from
America. It seemed like a fitting tribute under the
circumstances. Carla had jumped up on stage with him
and was now screaming out the chorus in her strong
Scottish accent.

Margaret, Gary, Lucas and Ellis where sitting in one of
the booths watching on.

Gary had never seen his brother so drunk, "I don't think
Marcus is dealing with his marriage breakup that well"

"Why do you think that?", Margaret was still clapping
along to her son's out of tune singing.

"Come on mam", Gary couldn't believe his mother
couldn't see the signs, "he's up singing, and he's
knocking back the pints pretty fast"

"His father just died", Ellis added. She didn't know Marcus at all before today, but she could easily understand why he was trying to let go.

"Exactly", Margaret was delighted to have a little female backup on her side for once, "your brother is hurting, and he's just trying to let go for the night. No harm in that"

"What about Cindy then, mam", Gary couldn't forget the teenage girl that once stole his brother's heart. Mostly because it was his fault that it had all fallen apart.

"Don't remind me about that little witch", Margaret had originally liked Cindy, but that had quickly changed as she led her son on.

"I remember that one", Lucas had a sharper mind than most, and few characters from his past would drop below the radar, "quiet girl if I remember correctly. Dark hair with glasses"

"Little bitch that broke Marcus's heart", Margaret knocked back a shot of Sambuca that had been sitting in front of her for a good ten minutes.

Ellis was totally confused by all this, "who is Cindy, and what has it got to do with Marcus's marriage to Celeste?"

Gary leaned over the table to be a bit more discrete, which wasn't really working since he still had to talk pretty loud to be heard over the music, "Cindy was this girl that lived down the street from us. Marcus was besotted with her, and everyone thought at the time that the feelings were mutual. Both of them were virgins and Cindy had told poor Marcus that she wanted to lose it to him. So my poor deluded little brother did everything to make sure she would stay with him. Spent all his savings on her, brought her out for meals that he could barely afford. Bought her clothes. Now, don't forget that he was only seventeen at the time and she was sixteen, if I remember correctly"

"Fifteen", Margaret corrected her son, "turns out she was lying about her age as well"

Gary tried to hide his discomfort. He'd always been under the impression that Cindy had been legal tender when he popped her cherry for the first time in his brother's bed. He was twenty three at the time and had always wanted to break in a virginal young lady like Cindy. She was nothing special to look at, in his opinion, but the idea of an untouched fanny in need of a good grand opening, was more than the encouragement Gary needed to sink his purple headed warrior deep inside her, for all of five minutes, while Marcus had gone to the shops to buy her cider. What once was a nice little sexual experience to reminisce about, was now quickly becoming a nightmare.

"Still don't get what this has to do with Celeste", Ellis protested.

Gary struggled to get to grips with the current conversation and pushed the negative thoughts to the back of his mind, "Marcus has got that same look in his eyes as he had straight after Cindy broke the bad news to him that she was no longer a virgin and didn't want to see him anymore. So Marcus went off, got really fucking drunk and slept with one of my mother's battered looking friends. One tooth Tina I think her name was. Isn't that right mam?"

Margaret took another large gulp of her double vodka and coke, "don't fucking remind me. Bitch tried to sell her story to the National Enquirer, but thankfully they didn't want it. Well, not for the amount of money she was asking for anyway. They found some other family scandal on Celeste's side to help commemorate their one year anniversary of marriage"

"Why weren't you two at his wedding?", Lucas had been listening carefully the whole time, and that was a question he had always wondered about, since seeing Marcus's wedding photos in the tabloids, and now seemed as good a time as any to ask.

"It was one of those spur of the moment things", Gary tried not to show it, but deep down he would have liked to have been part of that whole event, "Marcus popped the question and Celeste got all fucking excited about when the actually marriage was gonna be. She couldn't hold her piss for months on end, so decided for them both that they were getting married in Vegas. By some tacky Elvis impersonator if I remember correctly.

Honestly, who in their right minds would wanna get married by someone dressed up as the bloated and half dead king of rock and roll?"

Margaret's hand went up, slowly followed by Lucas, and then finally Ellis with a nervous smile, "I think it would be kind of cool to get married like that. Beats the boring traditional Catholic ones with have here. If I'm getting married, I want it to be somewhere sunny, with loads of my family and friends in attendance, and the most important thing of all, is a free bar"

Gary raised his glass for a toast, "I'll drink to that"

Lucas second that motion. Then Margaret and Ellis added their glasses to the rest, with much delight.

Ellis felt a part of a real family for once.

Rory was over at the bar, spouting out his feelings for Katie to an uninterested Bernard, "I think she liked me. You seen the way she smiled at me. There was something definitely there. I'm not being deluded. Am I?"

But Bernard wasn't listening, as his eyes were focused on the bare crossed legs of one of the younger town bikes, that was with a group of male (friends). Most likely just trying to get her drunk and out of her head on an assortment of drugs, just so she would put out to the lot of them at the same time. Bernard was pretty sure her name was Eva, but most fellas called her Easy Eva, because her knickers spent more time down than up. But tonight Bernard was pretty damn sure that the young woman didn't have any on, and there was rumours going around the pub that she didn't shave her muff, and that her natural hair colour was actually red.

"Are you what?", Bernard tried to keep his eyes focused on the young woman's bare thighs.

"Am I being stupid in thinking that there might be a chance with Katie?", Rory noticed where his friend was looking, "don't tell me your trying to see up her skirt again. That one is young enough to be your daughter"

"Young enough, yes", Bernard noticed that Easy Eva was doing a Sharon Stone with her legs, and never once dragged his eyes away from her thighs, "but she's not my daughter and that's the main thing. Never shagged her old battle axe of a mother"

"Her mother is younger than us", Rory laughed, "I'd say by nearly four years"

"I've already stopped listening to your negativity", Bernard was still studying that black little area at the meeting point of Easy Eva's thighs. It was growing wider as she unfolded her legs. Then there it was, a big mound of reddish pubic hair, and just as quickly as it appeared, it was gone again, as she refolded her legs the other way. Bernard swivelled around to the bar and thumped it triumphantly, "told you she wore no knickers, and that she has a big red muff on her"

"I'm god damn happy for you", Rory gestured to the young barman for another round of drinks for the two of them.

Bernard's mind had been put at ease and now he felt ready to try and help his friend, "look, if you fancy the tight little arse off that Katie one, then just fucking go for it tomorrow. You're never gonna see her again if it all goes to shit. I'm not saying that you have a good chance of her saying yes, but at least you'll have peace of mind that you tried. Never put off until tomorrow, that can be done today"

"Then why did you tell Franklin last week, that we couldn't get his job finished until Monday, even though there was fuck all left to do?", Rory knew the answer already, but he just liked to catch out his friend whenever he could.

Bernard patted his friend's back playfully, "why do in a week, what can be dragged out for ten fully paid days. Now, I'm gonna be watching tomorrow, and I better see you putting in some hard graft to get into that young one's knickers. Have you got that?"

Rory wearily nodded and went back to his pint, as he tried his best not to look at the old man staring back at him from the mirror behind the bar. A regular unwanted reminder that his age was quickly catching up with him.

Marcus and Carla finally finished their song and were making their way back to the rest of their group when Carla spotted a potential shag. The target was a long blue haired girl who looked in her early twenties with a slim build. She was dressed in fish net stockings, denim shorts and a colourful bra that was masquerading as a top. She was heading for the smoking area out the back of the pub. A poorly made, timber framed, seating area, that was a potential fire hazard thanks to all the cheap boat varnish that the owners of the pub had painted it with.

"I sense a bit of potential muff diving on the horizon tonight", Carla stopped in her tracks and fixed her hair with a comb that she liked to keep in her pocket at all times. Made her look like a modern day Fonz from Happy Days.

"You sense a bit of muff diving all the fucking time", Marcus joked. He'd caught sight of Carla's potential bed partner for the night and he had to admit that the young woman was definitely attractive.

Carla playfully jabbed the end of the comb into Marcus's chest, "you should be more like me and play the field while you still have a bit of youth left in you. Celeste is making the most of her time back home with Chad and her dopey friend Tory. You should be doing the same thing here. Live a little. Just like I'm about to", and with that, Carla slinked off out into the smoking area, leaving Marcus to return to the table alone.

When Marcus arrived back at the table, he found his mother questioning poor Lucas about his life. It was obvious the guy was gay. There had always been those rumours about him when they were growing up. Marcus easily could guess that was probably the reason his older brother gave his childhood friend such a wide berth in later years. Pretty cruel thing to do when he looked back now, but Marcus could understand Gary's reasons. They had grown up in a rough area of the north side of Dublin, and you had to do anything and everything to survive. That included cutting away anything that might drag you down or make you a potential target for bullies, verbal or physical.

"So what did you study in college?", Margaret was taking the lead in the investigation of where Lucas had been for all these years.

"I started studying art", Lucas replied, as he played with the small colourful straw in the barman's poor attempt at a whiskey sour, "but that wasn't really for me, so I took up fashion design in the same college and it turned out I was pretty damn good at it. Then I got a job with a fashion label up in Belfast and I never came back"

"Isn't it not dangerous up there?", unfortunately Margaret was still thinking in the past. Hard to forget the troubles of the seventies and eighties.

"It's not like that anymore", replied Lucas, "Belfast is a lovely place to live"

"But I'd say there's parts that are still a no go?", Gary asked.

"There is places you don't go on the outskirts of the city, but there has been times I've ended up in them after a night out", the smile grew wider on Lucas's face, "homosexuality doesn't know religious or political boundaries"

"Always knew you had to be gay", Margaret announced proudly, as if she just solved some major mystery that had been troubling top investigators for years.

Marcus, Gary and Lucas stared at Margaret like they couldn't believe she was only catching up now.

"What fashion label do you work for?", Ellis's voice cut through the silence.

"It's called Blossom", Lucas replied, 'it doesn't make clothes that are specifically suited to just men or women. We like to think that all our clothes can be worn by both sexes. They're colourful, bold and helps the wearer stand out from the crowd"

"Sounds like something my wife would wear", Marcus knocked down the last of his pint and soon started work on his fresh one.

"If only", Lucas replied, "if we got a big name like Celeste to wear our brand, we'd be catapulted right to the top. Unfortunately that's easier said than done"

"Maybe you could have a word with her", Ellis suggested to Marcus.

"I can't even get my wife to stop fucking around with other people, what chance would I have in getting her to wear one of Lucas's outfits", Marcus couldn't even look at the other people at the table. It was hard enough to say those words out loud, but now he wanted to take them back just as quickly.

Margaret rubbed her son's shoulder, "at least you're home with us for now", it was only then that she realised that there was one of their group missing, "where's Carla gone?"

Outside in the smoking area, Carla was doing pretty well with the young blue haired woman whose name turned out to be Pamela. She was a fitness instructor and was buzzing out of her head on ecstasy. Carla had opened up the conversation with the request for a cigarette, and then moved onto some light flirting. Soon that led to heavy petting, as Carla's fingers made their way up Pamela's skirt and into her knickers.

Pamela finally came up for some much needed air, "this can't be happening. I'm straight for god sake", she weakly demanded.

Carla stared into her eyes, "so is spaghetti, until it gets wet", before sinking two fingers deep inside Pamela, who proceeded to let out a long pleasure filled moan of delight.

Looked like Carla didn't have to go back to her hotel room alone tonight.

Chapter Fourteen

The corridors of Heavenly Celeste's home echoed loudly from her moans of delight as she rode Chad's open mouth like a over ambitious cowgirl who had something to prove. His expert tongue reached places deep inside her that few men had ever achieved.

Tory was perched naked on top of Chad's impressive erection, facing her best friend. They'd been taking turns for the last hour, and all involved were starting to get tired. Especially poor Chad who hadn't had a line of coke in the last hour. He needed the rush more than any of them, to keep the fire burning in his boiler.

But even with all the sex, drugs and excitement that Celeste was feeling, it still didn't hide that nagging doubt that was growing in the pit of her stomach, "I miss Marcus", she tried to stifle her next mini orgasm, but a moan still slipped out with her words.

"Why?", Tory was struggling to speak as well.

"Because I love him", Celeste had said those words so many times and to so many different people, Marcus included, but she'd never really had the emotions to back them up. Now there was something there. A feeling of loss. A feeling like she actually ached to be in Marcus's company again. No man had ever made her feel that way and it was confusing.

"You love everyone", Tory struggled to fight back another knee shaking orgasm, but the want got too much for her loins and she spurted her fanny juice all over Chad's already dripping cock.

"I know I do", Celeste was annoyed that her friend had stated the obvious, but this feeling was definitely more than that, "but me and Marcus aren't like that. We have something stronger than most. Why couldn't I see that until now?", she searched her mind for a reason, but it wasn't forthcoming.

"I'm no expert", Tory bit her lip and hoped she could get through her next sentence without another orgasm distracting her train of thought, "but I watch a lot of those daytime shows like Dr Phil and all those other cheap imitators, and what I think is wrong with you is that you couldn't see what you had until it was finally gone. But honestly Celeste, you and Marcus are so different as people. You'd have to give up a lot to keep him, and that's not the type of person you are. Besides, why make yourself unhappy, just to keep Marcus"

"There has to be some common ground that might suit us both", replied Celeste.

"Like what?"

"Honestly, I don't know, but I still have to try", Celeste checked her watch, "I have enough time to get to Ireland for his dad's funeral. Wanna come with me?"

"I'm coming with you here right now", protested Tory as she orgasmed once again.

"I mean to Ireland", Chad's tongue flicked into an unsuspecting moist crevice, deep inside her wet pussy and it sent a strange little tingle through Celeste's whole body.

Tory shrugged her shoulders, "okay then"

Chapter Fifteen

Jacinta's wine bar and gastropub was an upmarket establishment in the middle of Dublin. It was down near the docks and boasted a spectacular view of the Liffey and the convention centre. Dolly had decided that the place would be perfect to host a small get together of twenty or so close family members and friends. She really didn't wanna go home that night and had booked a room in the Gresham for the next few days.

Dolly was moving between groups of people as she played the perfect hostess, all the time trying to hide the pain and sorrow that was bubbling up from deep inside her. She and Mattie had drifted apart over the last few years. Barely sharing the same bed anymore, or even socialising in the same circles, but that didn't stop Dolly from loving Mattie any less. She just didn't know how much until now.

Cilla suddenly pulled Dolly aside, towards a discreet area of the private lounge that she'd hired for the night, "what is he doing here?"

Dolly wasn't sure what her sister was on about and glanced around the room at all the faces in attendance. No one jumped out at her straight away. That was until she spotted Trevor standing near the bar wearing a poorly fitting suit and clutching a glass of free Prosecco, "for fuck sake"

"Fuck sake exactly", Cilla fired back, "Trevor is the worst kept secret in this family and now you have him here at this get together, the night before you bury your husband. That's pretty messed up"

"I didn't invite him", Dolly protested.

Cilla tried to keep the false smile plastered across her heavily made up face, "get rid of Trevor before Sophie sees him. She'll fucking freak. The poor girl kept it quiet for you long enough, and you're lucky it isn't Ellis that knows your dirty little secret, or Mattie would have learnt the truth a long time before the poor man died. Now go deal with it and I'll keep Sophie occupied", and with that, Cilla stormed off in the direction of her niece.

Dolly tried to play it cool as she approached the handsome young man. Trevor was only twenty five, built like a tank and had a tan that belonged on a beach in Australia. He towered over Dolly and that's what she loved most about him. He easily could lift her up and penetrate her wanting body against any piece of furniture that took his fancy. He knew how to satisfy a woman of her vintage. Just a pity that each meeting came at a price. A price that was steadily rising with each month.

"What are you doing here?", Dolly spoke through a false smile as she checked her surroundings for listening ears.

"Just wanted to share my condolences with you", Trevor had a smirky grin plastered across his chiseled face.

"You and I both know that's bullshit. So why are you here?"

"Was in town and thought you might like to meet up tonight. I doubt you wanna be alone at this difficult time", Trevor stared into Dolly's eyes with that look he liked to do before touching her in ways that excited her.

Dolly felt a fanny flutter shoot up through her body. Which was then followed by a wave of guilt, "please, you can't be here"

Trevor discreetly held her hand in his, "where would you like me to be then?"

Dolly opened her handbag, pulled out her room card for the hotel and handed it to him, "room 406. Charge anything you want to the room and I'll be back later. Just please go now before Sophie sees you"

Trevor took the card and placed it in his jacket pocket, before kissing Dolly on the cheek and keeping her head there longer than necessary, "you know what your daughter's problem is. She's missing out on the cock action that all young ladies need. That's why you never see a happy lesbian", he then proceeded to run his tongue up the side of Dolly's face before pulling away, "see you later"

She watched on as her expensive lover left the function room. Dolly knew she should have been angry and upset about the way Trevor treated her, but she found it a turn on. Dolly had such control throughout the rest of her life, that it felt new and exciting to be treated like a doormat by such a young and hunky specimen of a man.

Cilla had blamed her sister's new weird sexual kinks on the fifty shades of grey novels, but Dolly knew it went deeper than that. She always wanted to be someone else's submissive sex slave. It was only in her later years that she tried to realise her fantasy. Now she was deeply regretting that decision.

Thankfully Sophie had seen none of that. She was sitting on the far side of the room, cradling a double vodka between her fingers. She had so much on her mind and so little amount of time to make sense of it. Besides dealing with her father's untimely death, Sophie was trying to come to terms with what had happened the previous night. It was all such a blur. One memory diluted into another, leaving them making very little sense. She'd had sex with a man the previous night. Only problem was, Sophie had little memory of which one of her friends it was.

"Last night was a bit weird, wasn't it?", Sophie hoped that Zara might be able to fill in some of the gaping holes in her own memories.

"It was different, I'll give it that", Zara was equally reluctant to talk about what happened.

"Always said that I'd never be intimate with a man, and now that I've crossed that line, I can't even fucking remember it"

"It had nothing to do with intimacy", Zara held her fiancé's hand in her own, "it was just four people trying to make a baby. I got no enjoyment out of having them inside me, and I'm pretty sure they felt the same way. Sebastian and Marco spent more time with each other, if I'm remembering correctly"

"Both of them!", this was the first time that Sophie had become aware that Zara had been with both men.

"That was the plan", Zara talked about the four way as if it was a business transaction, "we slept with both guys, and hopefully something comes out of it. This will all be for the best if we get our little bundle of joy. In one year's time we could be looking back on all this with our beautiful baby boy, or girl, in our arms. Isn't that a small price to pay for losing that part of our virginity to a man?"

"I guess so", Sophie reluctantly nodded in agreement, before knocking back the rest of her double vodka in one go, "I'm gonna go the bar for another drink. Want anything?"

Zara kissed the back of Sophie's hand, "no thanks, I've got everything I need with you"

Sophie didn't reply and just made her exit from the table, leaving Zara behind to contemplate if the previous night was such a good idea.

The small bar was packed with relatives, friends and business associates of Mattie's. Sophie was hoping not to be recognised as she slinked through the many suited people towards the edge of the bar. She ordered her drinks and proceeded to try and hide her face from all the people around her. Draping a few fingers over her forehead as she leaned on the shiny silver topped bar.

A hand brushed by and discreetly squeezed her ass before moving on. Sophie had a good fucking feeling that Frank was on the prowl again with his walking stick, so she tried not to look around and just waited for her order.

Then a firm hand pressed against her back. Which was then joined by a strong comforting shoulder. Sophie turned and came face to face with a smiling Sebastian. Even though she felt embarrassed and awkward to see him, Sophie still threw her arms around Sebastian's waist and buried her head in his firm chest. Tears began to stream down her face and into his good silk shirt.

"It's okay", Sebastian rubbed her hair caringly, "just let it all out"

Sophie sensed that other people at the bar were now watching her outburst, but thankfully Sebastian shielded her weak moment by putting his large body between her and everyone else.

The barman put Sophie's drink on the bar and without thinking she knocked it off the head, "can I get another please?"

The barman took the empty glass and wandered off to refill it.

"The last thing you need is to get blind drunk tonight", Sebastian picked up a glass of Prosecco from a silver tray that was sitting on the bar. He figured it was complimentary, "I know you're hurting, but drink and drugs just make it worse"

"It helped me to get through last night",; Sophie replied.

"Last night was totally different. We all wanted something, and the easiest way to get there was with the help of drugs and drink. Just hope we all get what we want. Good chance we'll end up with nothing at the end of it all"

"Good chance we could end up with two babies"

"Never thought of that", as if it only just dawned on Sebastian, what the outcome might be, "twins would be weird"

Marco appeared beside the two of them and started off an awkward group hug. He definitely wasn't dressed for a funeral with his pink shirt, with the top few buttons wide open, and his extremely tight white pants that made his package bulge out like a baby's head during child birth.

Sophie's eyes couldn't help but briefly gaze down at it. Unfortunately that left her with a sudden snippet of a memory that shot through her head, of a naked Marco slowly putting it inside her. Her own naked body tense across the bed as she gripped tightly onto the crisp white sheets with both hands. Thankfully the unwanted memory ended there and she dismissed it just as quickly.

Sebastian and Marco escorted Sophie back to the table were Zara was waiting. She noticed the tears in her fiancé's eyes and guided her back to her seat, "I knew you were bottling it all up", she hugged Sophie tightly, while kissing her dampened cheeks, "it's gonna be okay. Just breathe slowly and don't try to speak for the moment"

Sophie did as she was told and buried her face in Zara's shoulder for a while and listened to the three others talking between themselves. Their conversation was strangely normal in comparison to the turmoil that had set up shop in her own head. Sophie had always commented on other people who broke down and couldn't function after a family member's death. Saying that she'd never get like that under similar circumstances. Ellis was the weak one, not her. What in god's name was happening?. None of it was making any sense anymore.

Dolly finally composed herself in the toilets with another layer of makeup and rejoined her sister and friends at a table that overlooked the Liffey. A rather well off businessman and local politician called Nigel Lanson had made it his business to get close to Dolly. Shoehorning himself in beside her at the table. Not an easy task with his massive frame and girth. Once known for his Love Island contestant looks. Now he just looked like a contender for Weight Watchers. He had long grey hair that was tied into a neat ponytail. Most people reckoned he was hiding a growing bald spot underneath it all.

"This has to be a terrible time for you", Nigel spoke discreetly into Dolly's ear, "I'm sure you are aware, that I lost my wife under similar tragic circumstances"

"I thought your wife fell off a yacht in the Canary Islands?", replied Dolly.

Fell, being the most disputed word in all that. Some reckoned she was pushed because Nigel's businesses had been struggling at the time, and he just so happened to have a rather hefty life insurance policy taken out on his wife of twenty two years. It amazed a lot of people that the voting public could brush such sordid details about a political candidate's past, under the carpet, when lied to about the property tax finally being abolished. That turned out to be a load of bollocks as well. Nigel had actually voted to try and get it increased.

"Yes, she did fall off a yacht", Nigel smoothed back his hair, "but it was a tragic death like your husband's. They didn't find her body either. I never got the closure that you'll be receiving tomorrow"

"If you call burying a coffin full of bags filled up with parts of my husband as closure, then you and I have very different meanings of the word", Dolly tried to keep her confident tone in her voice, but it was quivering at the thought of what might be in her husband's coffin.

"At least he left you with a lot of businesses to keep you and the girls going to the end of days. Nice little nest egg for the whole family", a creepy little smile spread across Nigel's face as he spoke.

"Businesses that I haven't a clue on how to run", Dolly had always been the perfect hostess for her husband's dinner parties or public engagements, but she'd always left the business side up to Mattie. He had the head for all those numbers, "besides the vending machines stuff, he also had some tanning shops and a massage parlour"

"You do know that wasn't you're average massage parlour?", Nigel's voice dropped even lower.

"What are you trying to imply?", Dolly had her concerns at the time, about her husband buying a seedy massage parlour, but she had gone to the premises before he'd bought it and found this rather quiet Chinese family working there. There was five generations of them doing various styles of massages for their many customers.

Dolly hadn't seen any problems in her husband buying the business.

"I'm implying that the most popular service requested in that establishment, is a happy ending", Nigel smiled widely as he shared such sordid details, "but you don't have to be worrying about such things because I'd be willing to take it off your hands for a very good price. Maybe we could come to an agreement on all your businesses. You could unload the lot in one large piece and then you can go live your life in whatever manner you feel fit. Why spend your autumn years worrying about what once was Mattie's problems"

Dolly felt that this was all moving to fast, but it was tempting. She really didn't wanna take over her husband's problems, but she definitely didn't trust Nigel that much either. He may have been a good friend of Mattie's, but he was a sleazy fucker all the same. Probably a frequent user of her husband's Chinese massage parlour, if the happy endings were true, "let me think about it for a few days", that would give her a bit of time to think about his offer.

Nigel pulled out a business card from inside his jacket pocket and handed it to her, "call me if you change your mind", and with that, he got up and said his goodbyes to the other people at the table.

Dolly studied Nigel's business card. It definitely wasn't cheap. The raised print was on a gold painted card. It even had a nice smell of expensive aftershave off it.

Selling up was extremely tempting, but selling it to Nigel seemed like a risky decision. He was dodgy as fuck and Mattie kept separate from Nigel when it came to any sort of business. Dolly wasn't sure if she should follow her husband's example and do the same.

Chapter Sixteen

It had been a long day for Spencer Cruise. He'd searched various fields up and down the area where Mattie had been killed, but there was still no sign of his elusive head. Unfortunately sunlight wasn't on his side and Spencer found himself having to retreat back in the direction of his car for a few hours. There was nothing else he could do for now with the lack of sunlight.

As he crept through the bushes towards his car, Spencer became aware that there was other cars parked in the area. One or two of them had there headlights on and there was a group of men hanging around one car in particular. They all seemed to be playing with dices, or something similar.

It was only as Spencer discreetly crept a little closer that he noticed that it wasn't dice they were playing with. The men were furiously wanking away beside the open back window of a particular car. Inside was a couple doing it doggy style. The large black man bent over his small white lover. Their love making noises filled the cold night air.

Spencer just wanted to get back to his car that was parked in the far corner, but he feared being seen by any of the rough looking men, so he sat down and watched the weird show as it unfolded.

It was then that the woman stuck her head out the car window and began to suck off each wanking fella in turn. Their cocks slipping in and out of her mouth with ease.

Spencer recognised the woman involved. It was his beautiful Michelle. But it seemed like some grotesque copy of the women he loved. His beautiful wife would never degrade herself like that. Not his Michelle. Not her of all people.

But it was his precious Michelle, and Spencer soon came to realise that his marriage was truly over.

Chapter Seventeen

The loud squeals of a woman, alerted Dolly to there being someone else in her hotel room besides her lover Trevor. She braced herself, tapped her room card against the locking system and stepped into the room.

Dolly was met with the sight of a young naked blonde woman gyrating on top of a smiling Trevor. Her obviously fake boobs stayed rigid throughout their energetic, sweat soaked, sex romp.

Trevor spanked the young woman's ass playfully and ordered her to, "pump it harder baby"

"What the hell are you doing?", Dolly so wanted to shout those words out loud for the whole hotel to hear, but decorum and personal privacy drove her to keep her outburst to a minimum.

The young woman stopped gyrating and looked Dolly up and down, "are you Trevor's grandmother?"

"No my dear", Trevor spanked the young woman's ass once more, "that's my ever giving cash cow that just keeps on giving. Who do you think paid for this luxurious room", he gestured around at all the gold fittings and thick colourful fabrics on show"

The young woman laughed, "I thought it was you silly"

Dolly sat down on a gold painted chair that was beside the window, "why are you doing this to me?"

Trevor kept his blonde friend moving slowly on his lap, "had to teach you a lesson my old dear. You were ashamed when I showed up to your little get together tonight. I don't like being treated like that"

"It wasn't a god damn party", Dolly blurted out, "I'm burying my husband tomorrow and that was all his family and friends in attendance tonight. What did you want me to do?. Invite you in and introduce you to my family as my bit on the side!"

"That's all I am to you", Trevor replied while running one of his fingers over the young woman's lips, who playfully licked the tip with delight, "just a bit on the side. Your sex toy for when you choose to finally play. I'm a young man and young men have needs. That's why I have good little friends with benefits like Tina here, waiting on the sidelines when my sex drive needs a proper working out. I think you should sit tight and watch a real sex expert like Tina here", Trevor forced himself further inside the young woman's happy place and she moaned with delight.

Dolly grabbed the open bottle of champagne from a nearby ice bucket and headed to the bathroom, "you may be able to treat me like shit whenever you want, but I won't be putting up with this, not now, not never. I'm gonna go have a bath, and by the time I get back, I want both of you gone out of this room, or I'll be calling security to drag the pair of you out. Have you both got that?"

Tina slapped Trevor's chest angrily, "you said she was a watcher. That she got off on this stuff"

Trevor fired the young woman to one side and stormed out of the bed after Dolly, putting his arm in the bathroom door before she had a chance to close it, "don't you dare walk out on me", he pushed it open and blocked any escape she might have thought about.

Dolly sat on the edge of the giant bathtub and took a swig from the champagne bottle, "I don't need you anymore Trevor. Took my husband's death to see that. I'm not afraid of you and what damage you might be able to do to my good name, because none of that shit matters anymore. Pity I couldn't see that years ago"

Trevor got down on one knee in front of Dolly and changed his personality disturbingly quick, to someone who sounded liked they actually cared about other people's feelings, "please don't speak like that my love"

Dolly let out a short, sharp mocking laugh before taking another drink from the bottle. She'd played this game too many times with Trevor before, and she knew were this was going already.

But Trevor persisted. Running his hand along her thigh, up under her dress, and before Dolly had a chance to complain, he pulled her underwear to one side and forced his fist inside her.

Dolly tried to pull away, but Trevor grabbed her around the back with his free hand and pulled her close to his own sweaty firm body. He proceeded to pump his moist fist deep inside her.

"Stop that", Dolly moaned as she tried to fight off the growing urge to orgasm.

But Trevor didn't listen as he began to move his fist in and out of her roughly. Kissing her neck with delight, "just give into your desires baby"

And with that, Dolly orgasmed loudly. Her moans echoed around the bathroom, but Trevor wouldn't leave it there and kept on moving his fist in and out of her with much more force until she had orgasmed another four times.

Trevor sat Dolly carefully back down on the bathroom floor and kissed her lips gently, "now let me get rid of Tina and I'll come join you in that nice big bath in a minute. Then I'll help you forget about all this silly break up talk you keep going on about", Trevor got up and headed back out into the bedroom, closing the door tightly behind him.

All Dolly could do was sit on the bathroom floor and cry, as she listened to the moans of Tina in the next room. She was disgusted at her own weaknesses when it came to Trevor. Tonight she had come so close to driving him out of her life for good, but she'd fallen at the last hurdle. Life couldn't get any worse than this.

Chapter Eighteen

Unfortunately for Gary, when Murphy's pub had shut for the night and everyone had been fired out on the street, he was left with one big problem. A very drunken Ellis.

He hadn't a clue where she lived, and it didn't seem right to go through Ellis's handbag looking for her details. So he did the next best thing and brought her home to his apartment.

Thankfully Gary had help from Lucas, who had agreed to come back to his place for a drink. The taxi driver had given both men a suspicious look, when they carried a near unconscious Ellis to his taxi and stuck her in the back. Most likely he thought that they were gonna rape her, or something along those lines. Gary had assured the man that Ellis was his little sister and he was just looking out for her. That seemed to relax the driver a little.

When they got back to Gary's place, the two men dumped Ellis in his spare bedroom and proceeded to the sitting room, where Gary started to make up whiskey sours in the kitchen, while Lucas studied the framed pictures on the wall.

"What's with all the framed movie posters?", asked Lucas as he studied one for the movie Air America.

"It's mostly our teens spread out across four walls", replied Gary as he broke an egg into each glass, "you should see the bedroom, it's all the babes from the nineties in there. From Kylie to your one out of 2 unlimited"

"Kylie Jenner?"

"Kylie fucking Minogue. Why would I put some overly botoxed nobody on my bedroom wall"

Lucas broke a sly smile, "only fucking with you", he took off his jacket and fired it onto the couch. The sleeves of his shirt were rolled up to the wrist, leaving bruising on both forearms quite visibly.

Gary noticed this, "what's up with your arms?"

Lucas quickly fixed his sleeves back down to the wrists, "had a fall the other day. Came down hard on both my arms. Pretty embarrassing really"

"Embarrassing, is trying to jump a cement bollard and coming down hard on the next one with your face", Gary could still remember the pain when his nose shattered that night, and the next ten hours in casualty as he waited to get it fixed. His mother had not been impressed because he had his grad later that week.

"Did you stay in contact with anyone from secondary?", Lucas took his drink and sat down on one of the two leather effect white couches that circled the centre of the room.

"Not really", Gary replied as he sat down on the couch opposite, "you see some of them around from time to time, but everyone moved on. Even me and you. You went off to Belfast and never came back, while I married Aisling and had three kids who don't even bother with me now. Sometimes I wonder why I even bothered bringing them into this world. How about yourself?. Did you have any kids?"

Lucas awkwardly played with the glass in his hands, "kind of difficult when you're in a relationship with a fella"

"So it wasn't just a phase then?"

"Far from it", Lucas sat back against the couch. His eyes never once meeting Gary's as he spoke, "told you back then that I was pretty sure that it was just men I wanted. So that's why I went to Belfast. New life and a new me. Finally could be myself for once. No voices from the past trying to knock my confidence"

"So who's the lucky fella?"

"His name's Austin. He's originally from America, but he moved over here full time about six years ago. He's only twenty eight, but we get on great most of the time"

"So you're basically a sugar daddy", laughed Gary.

"Please don't say that", replied Lucas, "it's a little embarrassing on nights out. Fellas thinking that I'm his older brother, or even worse than that, some even think that I'm his father. That has led to a few dirty looks when they've seen us kissing. But we've been going from strength to strength, and hopefully soon we'll be getting married", Lucas held up his hand to show a diamond encrusted ring on one of his fingers"

"Congratulations", Gary started to roll up a joint on the coffee table, "nice to see that relationships was at least for one of us"

"What happened with you and Aisling?", asked Lucas with genuine concern, "I can still remember how well the two of you used to get on. What went wrong?"

"Honestly, I couldn't keep my dick in my pants, and she caught me fucking around several times. Don't blame her for dumping my ass. I treated her pretty badly and barely spent any time with the kids. No wonder they don't bother with me these days"

"That must be pretty tough?", asked Lucas.

It is", Gary hated to even think about it, let alone speak about it, "especially when my dad started to help out Aisling. He played the role of the perfect father figure after I was gone. Maybe I wouldn't have been such a fuck up when it came to marriage and parenting, if he had of stayed with my mother and acted like a proper father"

"I know he wasn't my dad, and I don't know what the two of you went through exactly, but I met him on and off over the years, and one thing that I always remember about him, was that Mattie was always very supportive of me and that he stood up for me on several occasions when I was being bullied outside the school. I never forgot what he did for me back then. My own dad used to tell me to cop the fuck on, stop acting so girly and fight back. All that got me was a lot of black eyes and a few bruised ribs. Had to hide my own sexuality from my own family for all these years. I'm sure they know the truth, but since I rarely visit home these days and they never come up to Belfast, I don't have to bother even trying to cross that bridge", there was a long awkward silence between them, before Lucas finally asked a question he'd been holding off from asking for awhile now, "did you ever explore that side of your sexuality after me?"

"We were young and just trying out things", Gary lit up the joint and puffed away as a way of avoiding eye contact for a few moments, "never thought about it after that. Ended up marrying Aisling and it was all downhill from there on in. So no, I never slept with another man after you"

"Do you ever think about those times with shared together?. Because I do. Can't get it out of my head sometimes. We had something special", Lucas was starting to get a little watery eyed, but he discreetly rubbed them dry.

"Had, being the key word in that sentence", Gary handed the joint over to his old friend, "we were young and confused. Neither of us knew or understood the feelings and emotions we were both feeling at the time. I was sleeping with women as well at the time. You wouldn't even go there"

"That's because I knew it was you that I wanted back then", Lucas was starting to look a little flustered as he inhaled hard on the joint, "and I never did have sex with a woman after that. It's been men ever since. We were both each other's firsts and that has always meant a lot to me"

"Aisling was my first", Gary lit up a cigarette, "what happened between us doesn't count. That's not what losing your virginity is"

"Stop thinking like our parents did and start living in the now. We both lost our virginity to each other, and no matter what way you look at it, we were both each other's first. That might not mean anything to you, but it means a damn lot to me", Lucas glanced at his watch for effect and got up to leave, "I'm gonna head back to my hotel now. Need some sleep before tomorrow"

"You don't have to leave", Gary stood up as well, "we're just having a bit of a disagreement. No need to let it escalate more than it already has. Please stay and keep me company. That's what I really need right now"

Lucas already has his jacket back on and was now zipping it up, "maybe it's for the best that I just head off before we open up any more old wounds", he took the joint out of his mouth and handed it back to Gary, "better not walk out of here with this in my mouth. Your neighbours wouldn't be too impressed"

Gary lifted the joint out of his friend's hand. Feeling the warmth of Lucas's smooth skin as they gently touched. A strange sensation passed between the two of them as their eyes met.

"Do you feel that?", Lucas blurted out.

"I don't feel anything", sweat began to drip down Gary's back.

Lucas moved in a little closer. The joint still interlocked between their fingers, "then you won't mind if I do this then", and with that, he planted a kiss on Gary's surprised lips.

Gary pushed Lucas away and rubbed his mouth clean, "what the fuck are you doing?"

"I just thought that I'd make the first move", Lucas started to back away towards the door, "I'm really sorry. I'm just gonna leave"

But before Lucas had a chance to escape, Gary rushed forward and pinned him to the wall by his arms. Their faces only inches from each other.

"I'm not gay", Gary blurted out.

"I believe you", Lucas was scared for his own safety, "please let me go"

"It's just that....", Gary couldn't find the words to describe how he was feeling, so lunged forward for a kiss instead.

Lucas happily let himself be taken.

Soon their clothes were being torn off as each one searched for the other one's bare flesh. Gary guided Lucas towards the bedroom, as their hands struggled to undo each other's pants.

"Are you sure you want to do this?", Lucas blurted out between kisses.

"Just shut up and go with it", Gary shut the bedroom door behind them.

The drinking session may have ended, but the night was only getting started.

Chapter Nineteen

It was two in the morning and Rory and Bernard were making good time down the M50, in Rory's overly used work van. The motorway was mostly quiet, so Rory had already reached a high speed. Thankfully the cocaine he had recently sniffed up both nostrils had helped get his head together enough to drive home.

"I was watching that film Big the other night. You know the one with Tom Hanks", Bernard was still snorting coke up his nose off a copper coin.

"Good fucking movie", Rory's eyes stayed firmly on the road. Weird white lines were starting to appear all over the tarmac, and he found himself concentrating even harder to keep the van steady.

"And that little hottie was in it. You know the one with the curly hair and nice boobs", Bernard wasn't great with remembering people's names. Especially women, and more importantly, women he'd slept with, "Elizabeth Olsen, I think her name was"

"Elizabeth Perkins", Rory quickly corrected his friend, "Elizabeth Olsen was that witch out of the Avengers"

"I don't remember the Avengers having a woman called Elizabeth Olsen in it", Bernard thought hard for a moment, "there was Diana Rigg, Honor Blackman, Linda something or other"

"Thorson", Rory was quick to help.

"Are you sure?"

"Yes, it's definitely Linda Thorson"

"Right then", Bernard continued, "Linda Thorson and Joanna Lumley. Personally my favourites were Honor and Diana. I can still knock out a load thinking about either of them, especially when they wore those skin tight outfits. Women have it handy when it comes to clothing like that. They don't have any bulges downstairs to distract from the tits bulging out at the top"

"What if they were overweight, or had one of those big flappy fannies that bulge out?", Rory loved to annoy his friend when he found the perfect opportunity, "then you'd have bulges in all the wrong places"

"I'm not on about ugly or overweight girls. Just nice attractive women with perfect figures and fannies so tight that you can crack a nut with the flaps. Nearly got one tonight if you hadn't of cramped my style", Bernard opened the passenger window and lit up a cigarette.

Rory started to laugh, "fuck off. That girl had no interest in you"

"Why the fuck not?", Bernard demanded.

"Because she was good looking, and I guess only about nineteen. You have to come to a point once in your life and realise that the days of pulling hot young women is finally past you"

"I'll still be pulling young women as long as there's still desperate ones out there at one in the morning looking for some free drugs for the night. The right girls will do just about anything for coke. I've had my cock sucked by some of the snottiest little madams around Dublin, because they wanted my drugs and they knew the only way to get them was to put out"

"How would you feel if it was other fellas talking about one of your daughters like that?", it was an oldie that Rory had used many a time with his friend, but it never got old, so he just kept on pulling it out.

"When do I ever see any of my kids?. They don't bother with me and vice versa. If they're stupid enough to fall into bed with some dirty old fucker for a few grams of coke, then they deserve everything they get"

"Did you just described yourself as a dirty old fucker?"

It was only then that Bernard realised his mistake, "fuck you"

They rounded the next bend in the road, and there on the hard shoulder was a speed camera van. Unfortunately it was too late to jam on the breaks and lower the speed to below the designated limit.

Rory punched the steering wheel, "for fuck sake. That's another two fucking points on my licence. Two fucking more and I'll be off the road"

"Pull in", Bernard ordered.

"Why?", Rory was already slowing down as they passed the speed van.

"Just do it", Bernard demanded even louder.

Rory pulled the van in on the hard shoulder. Bernard jumped out and disappeared off back down the road towards the speed camera van. Rory wasn't sure how long his friend would be, so took the opportunity to look up Katie on social media. He guessed her second name would be Wilson, like the owner of the funeral home, and thankfully he was right.

There was a load of skimpy bikini photos from a recent girly holiday to, what looked like one of, the Canary Islands. If Rory had of been home right now, he definitely would have knocked one out. Katie was definitely stunning, and a little lady to match. A quality that he rarely got to enjoy in a woman anymore. It was pretty much just dirty slappers that were up for sex these days.

Rory hated to admit it, but Bernard was right when he said that the only way that Rory was gonna get someone decent looking to put out these days, was by offering them the use of his drugs if they came back to his place.

Katie wasn't that type of girl, and in a strange way Rory was glad she wasn't. Being unattainable made women ten times more attractive in his opinion.

The passenger door suddenly opened and Bernard jumped back in, "I was fucking trying to tell you about Big earlier, and you threw me right off. I was on about that Elizabeth Olsen one"

"Perkins", Rory corrected his friend once again.

"Elizabeth Perkins then", Bernard lit up another cigarette, "I was gonna ask you, if you were thirteen again, and you could fuck any older woman from back then. Who would you pick?"

But that wasn't what was on Rory's mind at that very moment. He had more pressing issues, "what did you do to the speed van?"

"I took off its number plates and stuck them on your van, so head for the slip road and get off the motorway, and we'll come back down the far side. We're gonna give those fuckers a taste of their own medicine"

Rory did what he was told and headed off towards the next slip road. He started thinking about his friend's earlier question, "but in Big, Tom Hanks became a thirteen year old inside the body of an adult, so you wouldn't really be thirteen if you fucked an older woman"

"But you'd have your thirteen year old mind in a body that's balls deep in Elizabeth Olsen"

"Perkins"

"Whatever, you'd still be balls deep in her either way. Wouldn't that have been fucking awesome", Bernard's thoughts were wandering to one specific woman, "I always wanted to shag Debbie Harry when I was a teenager. Decorated many a picture of her with my sticky load. It was kind of a stupid thing really, because all I did was just ruin her pictures. And this was back before we had the internet, so there was no such thing as downloading new ones. When I think back now, why the fuck did fellas spurt their love juices all over their favourite pictures?. I know it just wasn't me, because I've borrowed enough dirty magazines in my day to know that most men must be at it. I remember getting the latest Club magazine off one of my mates in sixth class, and that must have been covered in all my fellow classmates dried spunk. It was like some kind of modern art job"

"Maybe it's like a dog marking his territory", Rory suggested.

"Maybe", Bernard noticed that they were already coming down the slip road that led up to the location of the speed van, "put your foot down and run the shit out of this rust bucket"

"There's nothing wrong with my van", Rory protested.

"Just floor it"

Rory did as he was told and quickly picked up speed. They flew past the camera van at well above the limit.

But Bernard wasn't happy with just the once, "do it a few more times. Teach these bastards a lesson"

Rory did as he was told and headed for the slip road again

"I would have much preferred Daisy Duke", Rory's mind was wandering back to his youth.

"Your one out of the Dukes of Hazard?", Bernard asked.

"The one and only. I can still remember those denim shorts she used to wear, and the odd time you'd even get her in a bikini. Now that was good wanking material"

"What was her real name again?"

"Catherine Bach", Rory couldn't believe that he actually remembered that.

"Did you ever watch the movie version they did with that gobshite who keeps injuring himself on Jackass, and that other guy who drank cum in American Pie?"

"The one with Jessica Simpson?"

"That's the one alright", Bernard already had a tingling sensation in his pants thinking about that blonde hottie, "fine little arse on her, and those tits were fucking perfect. Don't know what they look like these days, but back then she was fucking stunning"

"She was good looking, but I'd much prefer the original one that did it", Rory was starting to feel the effects of the drugs wearing off and was starting to wish he was at home in bed, with YouTube on the telly showing the greatest sexiest moments from the original Daisy Duke. But if there was no such video he'd probably settle for Jessica Simpson since they'd been discussing her so bloody much.

"We will agree, to disagree", Bernard was getting tired as well, and they had another long day tomorrow.

They past the speed van another four times before they had enough for one night. Rory then dropped Bernard home before heading to his own place. Only problem being that Rory forgot to take the number plates back off when he got home. Instead he sunk in between his cold sheets, got his cock out and started furiously wanking off to some choice footage of the original Daisy Duke. He'd happily Elizabeth Perkins her any day.

Chapter Twenty

This morning was particularly more difficult than normal for Marcus to focus his eyes on the bedside locker. There was an assortment of used condoms, there packaging and the traces of cocaine use. He found his phone among the sticky mess and checked the time. It was earlier than he had hoped for.

Marcus glanced around the rest of the room for any comforting familiarities, but it soon became apparent that he wasn't at home. Then again, was it ever truly a home. Celeste's house was always hers and hers alone. He was just the interloper into her life for those wild few years, and that was all over now.

It was only then that he noticed the sound of a shower running. Marcus started to try and stitch together the events of the night before. There'd been a lot of drink, drugs and partying.

Marcus then noticed a used condom on the end of his dick. It's flappy bag of cum swinging around the end of his cock was strangely off putting. He pulled it off and fired it onto the locker to join its friends.

Suddenly the shower ended and then there was the sounds of someone drying themselves roughly. Marcus felt his body tensing as he awaited for his one night stand to enter the room. And that she did alright, as a young slim woman with blue hair came out of the bathroom door, totally naked and still dripping water all over the place. Marcus was pretty sure that her name was Pamela.

"Heya", she was fairly chirpy for that time in the morning. Young people normally were after a late night drug and drinking session. It was like water off a duck's back to them fuckers. Pamela proceeded to put back on her skimpy outfit, that would make a prostitute blush.

"Hi", Marcus gave her a little wave as he pulled the bedsheets up to cover his bare chest.

"I've never slept with a celebrity before", Pamela was already pulling on her fishnet stockings, "wait till I tell all my friends. They are gonna be so fucking jealous", she got up off the end of the bed and slipped on her high heels, "maybe I'll see you around sometime", and with that, she headed for the bedroom door.

Marcus spotted her underwear on the edge of the bed. A frilly pair of blue knickers. He picked them up and held them aloft, "you forgot these"

Pamela turned and threw him a cheeky smile, "they aren't my knickers, besides, I never wear the bloody things when I can avoid it", she then disappeared out the door, shutting it tightly behind her.

This left Marcus thinking even more carefully about the previous night, until something finally dawned on him, and he lifted the pile of crumpled bedsheets along side him. There, was a tired looking, and very naked Carla, lying beside him.

"Is she definitely gone?", Carla asked in a rather rough fashion that most others wouldn't get away with.

"Yeah", Marcus replied, for lack of anything better to say. His poor head already swimming in sexual misconduct violations with a staff member.

"Thank fuck for that", Carla knocked the sheets off the top part of her body, leaving her small, but extremely perky boobs, on show, "can't stand all that pillow talk stuff the next morning, especially with those part time lesbians. All they keep going on about is how they've never done this before and I'm their first experience with another woman. That little blue haired hottie had an expert little tongue on her that got into places that I didn't expect", Carla took a pull from her vape.

"Did we have sex?", Marcus was still trying to put it all together, but it wasn't getting any clearer.

"Don't you start as well", Carla sat up in the bed and put her back to the headboard, "it's only sex. We don't have to make a big fucking thing about it. You have a sore back, you go to someone who can massage it"

"A masseuse"

"Whatever", continued Carla, "you go to a barbers for your hair, and a foot doctor for your feet"

"A chiropodist"

"Whatever. What I'm trying to say is that if you need sexual release, why use your hand to solve the problem, when you can get another person to bring you to that sexual peak. That's what all three of us got out of last night. An orgasmic transaction on all sides. You shot your load several times, and me and Pamela fingered each other into a state of pleasure that his higher than any man can ever get me. The best of both worlds"

"I'm gonna have a shower", Marcus had heard enough. He swung his feet out of the bed and went to stand up. It was only then that he remembered that he was totally naked in front of his employee. He quickly grabbed a pillow to hide his modesty.

Carla laughed loudly, "will you cop on. I've seen it all last night. You were inside several of my orifices for god sake. Calm down and go have your shower"

Marcus rushed to the en-suite door, still clutching the pillow.

"Might join you in a minute", Carla joked.

Unfortunately Marcus didn't take it that way and locked the bathroom door behind him.

"I'M ONLY JOKING", shouted Carla, but the sound of the shower seemed to drown out her words. She took another drag from her vape, "that fucker really needs to lighten the fuck up"

Chapter Twenty One

Even though it was a good few hours before the funeral, Dolly had decided to get dressed into her black outfit for the day. She had especially bought the little black dress for her husband's funeral. It may have shown a lot of leg on the six foot model that the clothing was designed for, but on Dolly's shorter frame it looked a lot more respectable, especially when worn with her thick black tights, leather boots and furry jacket.

Dolly was still a little sore from all the sex the previous night. Trevor had been in his dominant mood and had been pretty rough. Just the way she liked it as always, but it still left her with an awful guilt that morning.

Dolly couldn't stop thinking about Mattie throughout the night. He may not of held a place in her bed, but he most definitely had a large spot in her heart. He'd been her rock for all these years and now she felt alone. Cast out on a sea full of danger and the unknown. She just couldn't let anyone know her vulnerabilities. If the vultures caught sight of that, they'd swoop in and pillage her assets like the greedy fucks they were known to be.

Dolly entered the breakfast room of the hotel and before anyone had a chance to offer her a table, she made a beeline for the coffee percolator and poured herself a rather large cup of its energy boosting liquid. One of the few things that gave her any solace in this world.

"Looks like someone is all dolled up for her husband's funeral today", came a familiar voice from behind her.

Dolly turned to see Margaret sitting at a small table with the remnants of a rather large breakfast sitting in front of her. She was sipping at a glass of orange juice.

Dolly couldn't believe her eyes, "who in their right mind let the likes of you in here?"

"My son decided to treat me to a little luxury while he is back home for his father's funeral"

"Beats the place you've been squatting in for the last while", Dolly regularly had people keeping tabs on those she considered a threat to her or her family. Margaret wasn't much of a threat in anyway, but Dolly still liked to be updated on how shitty the woman's life was.

"So you've been checking up on me", Margaret put her hand to her heart mockingly, "I'm so flattered Dolly. Nice to know you care"

"So tell me Margaret, which wonderful son of yours paid for all this?", Dolly was as bold as brass and sat down on the chair opposite. Leaning backwards to keep some distance from all the half eaten food sitting on the table. Last thing she needed was to get her dress dirty, "doubt it was the criminal and used car salesman, who I regularly see in the papers these days. What was his name again. Gary, that was it. What a disappointment he was to poor Mattie. He so wanted to help him out financially when it came to his third level education, but your son fired it back in his face. I wonder would he have been so rude if he knew his future would be selling used cars and getting mixed up with criminal gangs"

"My Gary chose his own path in life, and he's holding his own for now. That's all any parent wants for their kids. At least he wasn't a constant burden on Mattie's finances like your two little blonde bimbos", Margaret wasn't even sure if that was true, but it seemed like a pretty good guess all the same.

"My daughters both have their own jobs and now live their own lives. Anything my husband did for them was just a little extra on their already well secured futures", Dolly felt like she had the upper hand the whole way through the heated discussion with her husband's ex wife.

Margaret couldn't help but laugh to herself as she took another drink of her orange juice.

Dolly sensed something was off, "what's so god damn funny?"

"That you still call him your husband"

"Just because he's dead, doesn't make him any less my husband"

"That's not what I meant"

Dolly didn't like were this was going and leaned a little closer, so that no one else could hear her curse, "then what the fuck do you mean?"

"I've held my tongue for long enough. Protected Mattie and his new life for god only knows what reason", Margaret was starting to regret some of the decisions she'd made over her life.

"If you're trying to say that there's something illegal about my marriage, then you can fuck right off Margaret. I seen the annulment from the church. Your marriage to Mattie was done and dusted before I married him"

"That was a joke", Margaret was trying her best not to show any emotion as she thought about her marriage to Mattie, "how could the church annul a marriage of eight years, when there was two kids involved. Don't know how Mattie swung that one"

"So you admit it yourself", Dolly took the initiative and jumped on what Margaret had just said, "you were divorced and there was nothing wrong with mine and Mattie's marriage"

Margaret took a gulp of air as she debated whether or not to say the next piece of damning information, "Mattie lied to you about the legal separation. He'd left it too late before your marriage, that it hadn't gone through yet. The church had already signed off on it, and your big day was fast approaching, so he begged me not to say anything, just so that you could have your special moment with all your family. You don't know how hard that was for me and my sons. Having to sit at home in our shitty rented two bedroom home, as their father was off marrying you"

"If any of this shit was true", Dolly fired back, "you would have come at us years ago with it. No way you would have sat back all this time and said nothing"

Margaret stood up from the table and drank the last of her orange juice, "then you don't know me very well", and with that, she marched off out of the breakfast room.

Leaving a very confused Dolly with a lot to think about.

Chapter Twenty Two

Her phone had rang several times that morning already, but Ellis had been struggling to waken up and just ignored the cheery tone that kept playing over and over again. She was having sweet dreams of a life less ordinary. Kids, a husband and a beach in some mythical hot country were money wasn't required for anything, and the sun constantly beamed down on the blues seas that lapped the edge of the beach softly. She'd had this dream many times before, but never this vivid. It was like she was almost there. That her dreams were soon gonna become a reality.

Unfortunately all this came to an abrupt end when the phone vibrated off the edge of the high locker and bounced off the top of her head. Ellis tried to force her eyes open, but all she could see was blinding light streaming in from a nearby window. Her head was thumping pretty badly as well. It didn't take her long to remember the string of shots she'd been knocking back the night before. That wasn't like her at all. Ellis just hoped she hadn't made a show of herself the previous night.

A horrible thought ran through her tired mind. Had she been someone's one night stand. Ellis turned around in the small bed and thankfully there was no one beside her. An added bonus came from the fact that she still had all her clothes on from the previous night, even her shoes. Unfortunately now they were all badly creased and smelt of a mixture of stale alcohol and sweat.

Ellis put her feet out onto the floor and tried to make sense of what had happened the previous night. She'd been drinking in the pub with Gary and his family and things started to get a bit hazy after that. Thankfully a framed photo on a nearby chest of drawers filled in the blanks. It was a picture of Gary with his ex wife Aisling and their kids. It was definitely taken a long time ago, because his kids were still very young at the time. Ellis found it difficult to comprehend that those little kids were actually her nieces and nephew.

Suddenly her phone rang again and Ellis scrambled to find it on the fluffy carpet were it had fallen earlier. She picked it up to see that her boyfriend Steven was calling. Ellis knew that he wasn't gonna be impressed with her staying out all night, but if she wanted this relationship to work out, she had to be totally honest with him and vice versa.

Ellis nervously answered the phone, "heya"

"Where are you?. I've been calling all morning", Steven was fairly angry already.

"Went out for a few drinks with the family and one thing led to another…"

But before Ellis had time to explain herself, Steven cut her off, "don't start giving me bullshit excuses that you stayed in your mother's or Sophie's place, because I've been onto both of them this morning and neither of them knew where you were. That didn't stop them trying to cover for your ass"

Ellis didn't know whether the truth sounded any better, but gave it a try all the same, "I'm here in my brother's place. Remember I told you about him"

"You don't even know that guy Ellis", Steven fired back, "he could be some fucked up rapist or weirdo. Bet you were drunk out of your fucking skull again?"

Ellis hated being reminded constantly of her drinking habits, that she reckoned was fully under control. It looked like she now had to tell Steven the truth about how well she really did know Gary, "he's not a stranger Steven. I've been meeting Gary for a good while now. Meeting him for lunch in town. Didn't wanna tell you or the rest of the family"

"So you lied to me then?", Steven fired back.

"Seems a small little white lie in comparison to what you've been up to lately", Ellis didn't even know were the strength came from, but she embraced it with open arms.

"Please come home and we can talk about this", Steven pleaded.

Ellis took a deep breath and tried to steady her nerves, "I'll be home soon enough and we'll talk then, but don't even try and cause shit today of all days"

"I promise I won't"

"Okay then, I'll be home soon"

"Love you"

Ellis paused for a moment as the words lingered on her lips for a brief moment, "love you too", she then hung up the call as tears came to her eyes once more. A mixture of pain and anguish brewing from both her relationship problems and dealing with her father's death.

When she'd finally composed herself, Ellis left the bedroom and soon could smell fresh coffee being brewed. She felt like Hansel and Gretel as the smell lured her into the kitchen were Gary was burning toast.

"Morning", he smiled as she entered the room, "fancy a coffee?"

"That would be great", Ellis sat down at the table. As she glanced around the apartment, it started to dawn on her a little about what had happened the previous night, "I was really well out of it"

"That you were", Gary put on more toast, "but we all deal with grief in different ways. You had a strong bond with your father, so that's only natural"

"Our father", Ellis corrected him.

Gary wearily nodded in agreement, "he was our father. It's just that I didn't have the same bond with him growing up. Even Marcus was a little closer to him than I was"

"Paying for all his college courses", Ellis added.

"Exactly. It's not like he didn't try the same with me. He offered to put me through college and when I turned that down, he offered to get me a good job in one of his friend's companies. I knocked that back as well. I don't feel bad for doing any of that. I'm proud of were I've gotten myself on my own. Might be a shitty used cars business, but it's my business and that's what makes me so happy. I got here on my own", only then did his mother's words come back to haunt him, "well, I thought I'd did it all on my own until yesterday", Gary put a cup of fresh coffee in front of Ellis, along with a few slices of buttered toast.

Ellis gladly took a drink of the warm comforting liquid, "what does that mean?"

Gary sat down across from her, "turns out our father was throwing business my way secretly. My mother broke the news to me yesterday. Still don't know how to feel about that"

"It must show you that he really did care about you?", Ellis could see the hurt in her brother's eyes.

"I don't really know anymore. Thought I knew me and my own life. Now it's all making no sense anymore", Gary's mind was starting to wander back to what happened the night before. He'd had sex with Lucas and now he was questioning his sexuality once more. Something he hadn't done in over twenty five years. He tried to dismiss it all by quickly changing the subject, "less about me. How are you today?"

Ellis shrugged her shoulders, "same as I was yesterday. Only thing is that Steven rang me this morning. He wants to sort things out. I was wondering if there was any chance of a lift to my place?"

"I can drop you there after breakfast"

"Thank you"

It was then that Lucas wandered out of Gary's bedroom in just his boxers. He was stretching and yawning as his feet stumbled slightly on the carpeted floor, "morning", he announced.

"Morning", Ellis was a little confused about what was going on and looked to her brother for an answer that might make sense.

Gary slightly panicked and just blurted out the first thing that came to mind, "I let him have my bed last night, and I slept on the couch.

Ellis was too tired and sore to question it any further, so just replied, "oh right", she had enough going on in her own life that day, to be taking on anything else.

A short time later, Gary dropped off Ellis at her place and then he headed for Lucas's hotel in the centre of town. There had been a lot of silence between the two of them since Ellis had gotten out of the car. Neither being too sure of what to say to each other.

"Penny for your thoughts?", Lucas tried to make a joke of it, but he hoped Gary's answer would still be serious.

"About what?", Gary mumbled back as he avoided being the one to bring it up first.

"About us and what happened in your bedroom last night", Lucas was growing more and more annoyed that he had to practically spell it out for his old friend.

"What happened last night was some alcohol induced nostalgia. We were both feeling a bit horny, and there was no hot women around to turn my charms on, so you had to do. That's the end of it. I've got to bury my father today and the last thing I need in my ear is you whining on about how there might be something more between us. Well there's not. Last night was a mistake. Sooner you see that, the better"

The rest of the car journey to Lucas's hotel was done in silence. When they had parked out front, Lucas had offered Gary to come in while he was getting changed.

Neither said much to each other as they walked through reception and went up in the lift to the sixth floor.

The lift was narrow and both men found themselves staring into each other's eyes. Neither knowing what to say to the other. It was Gary who made the first move as he lunged for Lucas and kissed him passionately on the lips. His hands working there way inside his shirt. He pulled it up out of Lucas's pants.

Lucas had been taken by surprise and just went with the moment, letting Gary do whatever he wanted in the confined space of the lift. That was until the lift dinged open and the two men were met by a rather large group of Japanese tourists who looked even more surprised to see them and what they were at in the lift.

Gary made his apologies and pushed his way through the group, pulling Lucas by the hand behind him. They soon found Lucas's room and were safely inside before Gary spoke again, "now, where were we?"

But this time Lucas took the initiative and pushed Gary back against the door, "somewhere about here", before planting a French kiss on his old friend.

The two of them dragged and pulled at each other's clothing until both of them were soon naked and rolling around in the crisp sheets of the hotel bed.

Gary suddenly came up for air, "now don't forget, this means absolutely nothing"

Lucas just ignored his protests, "just shut the fuck up and kiss me?

Chapter Twenty Three

It had been difficult to find a perfect outfit for a funeral, but Jamie had been delighted with her final choice of clothing. A very short black skirt, a brassiere that showed off a good amount of cleavage and a jacket that was too small to shut at the front. Unfortunately the only shoes she could find to match were a pair of her mother's high heels, that were bright red and extremely shiny. Jamie admired herself in her full length bedroom mirror. If there was any talent at this funeral, she was confident that pulling them would be easy enough.

It still didn't make sense to Jamie why her mother was so eager for her to go to the funeral. Jamie didn't even know the guy. Some old friend of her mother's, and none of her sisters were asked to join them. Even more irritating was that the funeral was on the south side of Dublin, so an hour and a half of travelling each way on top of it all. The only plus out of all this was that Jamie's mother Ellen reckoned that there would be a free bar. That was most definitely tempting.

Her mother Ellen shuffled into Jamie's bedroom. She was also wearing a tight black skirt which was a little bit longer than her daughter's, but not by much. Her cleavage was bulging out even more than Jamie's, but her jacket was able to shut, so less was on show for now. That was until she'd get a few drinks in her and all bets were off.

Ellen spotted the red high heels on her daughter's feet, "they're my bloody shoes you cheeky little mare. Get them off"

"Jesus mam", Jamie protested, "they look better on me anyway"

"Don't you start today Jamie. We've got a long day ahead of us"

Jamie pushed the high heels off her feet with ease and kicked them over to her mother, "go on then, have them", she folded her arms angrily, "don't know why you even want me to go to this stupid funeral in the first place. Don't even know a fucking Barry Haystings"

"It's Mattie Jenkins", Ellen protested as she sat down on the edge of her daughter's bed and began to put on her favourite high heels, "he's an old friend of the family's"

"I don't remember him", Jamie started to search her wardrobe for another set of heels.

"That's because it was before your time on this earth", Ellen knew she had to say what had to be said, before they went out that day, "can you please sit down for a minute and I'll explain why"

Jamie finally found a pair of red leather boots that went up to the knee and reluctantly sat down beside her mother on the bed to put them on, "go on then"

"Well, you know the way I don't know who your father is"

"Yeah"

"Well Mattie is one of the potential fathers. I know that I can't be sure, but isn't it better to go to the funeral either way, just in case?"

Jamie was briefly lost for words, "so the only reason you're bringing me to this today, is because this old git that got blown up, might be my dad?"

"Exactly"

"For fuck sake mam, you could have broke the news to me a few days ago, not on the morning when they're about to bury the man six feet under"

Ellen lit up a cigarette as her nerves quickly got to her, "I'm sorry love, it was a difficult time around when you were conceived. Already had your two sisters, and neither of their fathers stuck around. That's when I decided not to be said and led by any one man anymore, so I started seeing a couple at one go. I was like Meryl Streep in Mamma Mia", that was how she liked to think of herself since seeing the ABBA song inspired movie.

"Mam, you were riding six men around the same time", Jamie had no problem with busting her mother's bubble, "and one of them was a gang bang with three of them.

That's not exactly something I wanna go around boasting about"

"Gang bang makes it sound so sleazy", Ellen had come up with a better way to describe it over the years, "I prefer to call it a group love cuddle. That sounds much better"

"Call it what you want mam, it's still a gang bang", then it only dawned on Jamie, "for fuck sake mam, please don't tell me that this Barry fella was one of the guys taking part in spit roasting you?"

Ellen tried to keep her cool, "his name's Mattie, and no he wasn't one of the guys that took part in my group love cuddle, and please don't use the words spit roasting to describe how you may have been conceived"

"Easy for you to say", Jamie took the cigarette out of her mother's hand and took a drag, "I've never had anyone to call dad"

"What about that fella you had in your room the other week?. He kept wanting you to call him daddy", unfortunately the bedroom walls in their house were rather thin.

"That's not even funny mam", Jamie had brought home a fella that was over ten years older than her, and covered with so much body hair that he looked like a rather muscular bear. He'd enjoyed doing Jamie doggy style, while spanking her firm ass and shouting, "who's your daddy?"

Ellen checked her watch. They hadn't much time left to catch the train, "look, we need to get going if we want to make it up here in time. I know this is all hard to take in, but it's best that you say your goodbyes, just in case Mattie is your father. Look on the bright side"

"Which is?", Jamie definitely couldn't see one.

"Unlike two of your sisters, at least you have your father narrowed down to six men. Poor Bethany was conceived at a Fleetwood Mac concert. Sneaky bastard said he was gonna get me backstage to meet the band. Turned out to be a fucking tramp, and Isabella was created over a car bonnet in Benidorm, so you shouldn't look at this as a bad thing"

Jamie was already tired from trying to make sense of all this and got up from the bed, "look mam, let's just go and get this done", she fixed her tight skirt back down.

"Good girl, I knew you'd see sense", Ellen jumped up and pulled her skirt down as well. She put her arm around her daughter's waist and admired their outfits in the mirror, "you can't deny that the pair of us are definitely hot to trot"

"That we most definitely are", Jamie couldn't deny that they did look pretty feckin awesome. Maybe some good would come out of today. Funerals normally meant grieving hot guys, and a free bar would mean they'd be drunk as well. Brilliant combination.

Chapter Twenty Four

"This shouldn't be fucking here", Mr Roberts had been overseeing the renovation work of the new section of the graveyard, and there hadn't been any problems until now.

They had carefully checked all the accompanying paperwork and maps before buying the adjoining piece of property, so it had come as a very big surprise to find a massive old rusty pipe running through the bottom of the very first grave they had dug.

Leonard, the apprentice gravedigger, tapped the pipe roughly with the end of his spade, "it's the real deal alright. Someone's fucked up somewhere along the line"

Mr Roberts studied the paperwork in his hands once again, "it should be marked down on the plan for the field"

"Maybe it's been abandoned. Just some forgotten old pipe work from a couple of hundred years ago. Was there ever any old ruins around here?"

"Whole place has always just been fields", Mr Roberts put his paperwork away and cleaned off the excess dirt on his pants, "don't touch anything for now. I'll be back in a few minutes. Gonna give the council a call", he hurried off.

Leonard was left alone in the six foot deep hole. He found himself studying the strange pipe once more. It had a bolted on metal cap in the centre that could easily be busted off if necessary. Leonard fought the urge to break it open, even though it seemed such an easy way to be sure if the pipe was now dormant.

Elsewhere in the graveyard, Margaret had wanted to see where the final resting place of her husband was gonna be later that day. She had a habit of visiting loved one's open graves before the burial. It gave her comfort somehow. Sneaking a few good luck charms into the bottom of the hole. Anything to help the journey to heaven, be a little more smoother.

Marcus and Carla had accompanied her as well. They were all dressed for the funeral already. Marcus had been avoiding any alone time with Carla since that morning. What had happened between them still felt totally wrong, and went against all employee and employer regulations. Last thing he needed was a scandal. His face was gonna be in the tabloids enough when the media found out about his and Celeste's breakup.

Marcus had actually been missing her. Something he hadn't honestly thought would happen. Celeste had been his rock since they first met. The person that pushed him to go bigger and better. Yes it might not had always worked in his favour, but she wasn't to know that. Just a pity he could never get used to her colourful past, or when it came back to haunt them. Celeste was a wild woman and was never gonna change. Marcus cursed himself for not seeing it long before they were married, but he reasoned with himself that maybe he did and just chose to ignore it. That made much more sense.

"Still don't get why you like to throw stuff in the grave Margaret?", Carla had been trying to make sense of the old woman's superstitious ways.

"It's just a family tradition that my great grandmother started, and it kind of made its way down through the family over the generations", Margaret pulled a handful of trinkets from her pocket that included a four leave shamrock and a one cent piece, "she said that people needed all the luck they could get when on their way to the afterlife. That always made sense to me"

"My family just love to cremate each other", Carla figured her own body would meet the same faith, whether she liked it or not, "even my uncle Roger set his house on fire with his wife in it. Stupid bastard was drunk and thought she was having an affair, so burnt the house to the ground"

"Jesus Christ", Marcus blurted out, forgetting all about trying to avoid conversation with his assistant for the moment, "was she okay?"

"She was grand", Carla replied, "pity her lover, who was hiding in the wardrobe upstairs, didn't come out a well. The guy was burnt to a crisp. People said he looked like a chicken nugget that had been left in the fryer for too long"

"That's a mental image that I don't need right now", Marcus tried not to think about it, but his mind kept going there.

Margaret noticed the open grave in the empty corner of the new section of the cemetery. She wandered over and glanced down into the six foot hole, to see a young blonde man sitting on a rusty pipe, smoking a large joint.

"What's going on here?", Margaret asked.

Leonard hid the joint behind his back and tried to blow the smoke out the side of his mouth, "nothing missus. Just smoking a cigarette", he fanned the cloud of smoke from around his head.

"Is this Mattie Jenkins plot?"

"Don't know missus, but it's the only one we're opening up today"

"What's with the pipe?", not exactly the first thing that Margaret expected to see in her husband's grave.

"No idea missus. We just found it while digging. The boss has gone off to check is it still in use. Have to wait here until he gets back"

Marcus cared little about the contents of the grave and pulled Carla aside while his mother was occupied, "is what happened last night gonna be an issue between us?"

Carla couldn't help from flashing him a cheeky smile, "the only person that's making an issue out of this is you. You don't see me overthinking all this. It was just sex Marcus. Just because I had your cock in my mouth for god only knows how long, doesn't change our working relationship or friendship for that matter. It only seems to be you that is making a big deal about all this"

Marcus knew she was right. He had to calm down about all this. It was just sex. Nothing more, nothing less. It was then that his mobile phone rang in his pocket. Not many people had his number, so Marcus figured it had to be important.

It was his agent Estelle Gandolfini, a small Jewish woman with a temper that scared most people, and she wasn't in a good humour, "what the hell is all this about a threesome Marcus?. It's all over the news here"

Marcus was surprised that Celeste's sex session with Chad and Tory had gotten out, but it didn't surprise him. There was always a member of staff willing to fuck any celebrity over for the right price. Estelle had always told him to tell her if any scandals ever cropped up in his life, but he hadn't the heart to ring her about Celeste. He was still trying to wrap his own mind around it himself.

"It only happened the other day, so I didn't think it would get out so quickly", Marcus really wasn't in the humour to talk about this, but his agent wasn't the type of person to respect his personal needs when financial gain was in danger for both of them, "besides, this is more on Celeste than me"

"What's Celeste got to do with this?", Estelle asked.

Carla's phone beeped in her pocket and she opened up the video file that a friend had sent her. It was of a young woman bouncing furiously on top of a hairy cock that sprung in and out of her back passage like a pneumatic drill.

"My ass looks amazing", Carla blurted out with much pride.

"Well, that's the main thing", Marcus sarcastically replied, his eyes still drawn to the small screen as the camera panned around the back of Carla to reveal that he was lying underneath his assistant. His eyes rolled back in his head and the sweat dripped off both their bodies. Then Pamela, who was obviously operating the camera, climbed on top of his face and filmed straight down her chest, through the ample valleys of her boobs, down towards her wanting crotch as Marcus's mouth could be clearly seen eating the young woman out, "this is fucking disastrous"

Estelle was still on the other end of the phone, "that's putting it mildly. The press is having a field day with the footage. Don't be surprised if the paparazzi show up at your father's funeral. Those maggots are like vultures, just waiting for the weak to mess up, and boy did you mess up big this time my friend. They'll be calling you a love rat next, and blaming Carla and that other woman for breaking up your marriage"

"I didn't break up shit Estelle", Carla wasn't taking that comment lying down, "they're already broken up"

"What's that?", this was the first time that Estelle had heard about the breakup.

Marcus threw his eyes up, before giving Carla a look to let her know that she had said too much already, before finally answering his agent, "me and Celeste are no longer. So you don't have to worry about that"

"That's perfect", Estelle was already searching her old fashioned Rolodex for the right numbers to call, "I'm gonna start working on damage control. Call you later", she hung up the phone without even a goodbye.

Marcus couldn't believe what was happening. He tried to ignore the moans of Pamela on the small screen, that Carla had decided to turn up the volume on, "this is not the type of fame I wanted in Hollywood. A low budget Tommy Lee and you're my Pammie"

"Always seen myself more as a Kim Kardashian if we're talking about celebrity porn stars", Carla was starting to wish that she had of gotten Pamela's number. The sex had been pretty awesome and well worth repeating, even if the little blue haired bitch had sold them out to the press, for most likely fuck all money. But Carla knew Hollywood better than most and was used to that sort of behaviour from people. That's why it was refreshing to work with someone like Marcus. He wasn't a dick like most of the filmmaker pricks who treated women like they were second class citizens and that they were only on set to make coffee and suck their sweaty dicks on command.

"I'm so fucked right now", moaned Marcus, "can't see life getting any worse than this"

"Just give it a good whack", Margaret was still trying to advise young Leonard on how to check the pipe to see was it still working, "I've worked around a lot of old pipes like that in the past and they're never still in use"

Leonard wasn't the sharpest tool in the box and slammed his shovel hard into the cap that was bolted to the top of the pipe. It flew off with surprising ease, followed by a thick brown liquid that shot up and got Margaret right in the face, firing her back onto the ground in a heap. The stinking fluid geysered up out of the plot, ten foot into the air and acted like a giant sprinkler as raw sewage sprayed down on Carla and Marcus.

Leonard jumped out of the hole as it started to fill with the smelly brown liquid. He knew he'd fucked up and was planning to put as much distance between him and the graveyard before Mr Roberts came back and seen what he did.

Carla spat out the raw sewage that had gotten into her mouth, "you were saying"

"I stand corrected", Marcus had unfortunately been proven wrong.

Chapter Twenty Five

It had been a long night for Spencer Cruise. He'd watched his wife getting gang banged for what felt like hours, and by the time all the cars and men had fucked off, it was nearly morning, so he'd only gotten an hour sleep in the back of the car before he had headed back out in search of his friend's head.

It was hard to see his wife in such complicated positions. They'd been both virgins when they had met. Now he couldn't see his beautiful Michelle as the beautiful innocent woman she once was. The image of her moving from one stranger's cock to the other's, haunted his thoughts. He'd most definitely lost her, but it still was gonna be difficult to say the words out straight. But they had to be said. No way their marriage could go on like this. Life wouldn't be worth living if it was all gonna be false and hollow. But that was a problem for later. For now Spencer had a mission to accomplish before he could worry about his own needs. Today was about Mattie.

There was one area along the river that he hadn't checked yet. It was mostly made up of high dense grass and had a raised hill that underneath housed a load of tiny caves that animals liked to use as makeshift houses for their young. He prayed the head might have ended up in one of these. Unfortunately the animal that took it may also be at home, but that was a risk he was willing to take.

He pushed his way through the long grass until he came to the clearing. The area was quiet and no movement was in sight. Spencer edged from hole to hole and glanced in quickly before moving on. The area smelt of stale shit and rotting flesh. He wasn't sure was that a good thing or not.

Spencer finally came to a larger hole near the end and froze on the spot when he came face to face with Mattie's badly damaged head. There was a lot of skin missing from the scalp and one of the eyes was hanging out of the socket. Mattie strangely still had a look of his old self to him, like he'd just had too much to drink and passed out in a corner.

As Spencer reached out to grab the head, a low snarling noise came from behind him. He turned around and came face to face with a fairly angry looking dog. It was big and covered in dirt. Probably had been living out by the river for a very long time. The dog's teeth were on show and dripping with spittle as it moved closer.

"Nice doggy, good boy", Spencer was trying to keep one eye on the psycho dog, while his right hand reached out and searched for the head. Slow movements were needed at all times and he'd heard something about maintaining eye contact with a wild dog. Well, he hoped that was what you were suppose to do in these situations.

Unfortunately he missed his friend's severed head and his fingers landed on something furry. Spencer instinctively turned his head to come face to face with another snarling dog. This one was even bigger than the last, and twice as angry looking.

"And you're a nice doggy too", Spencer was starting to feel that his life had finally ran its course. Maybe it was for the best. He had nothing left to give this world and a wife who didn't even love him anymore. Maybe it was best if it all ended like this.

But Spencer quickly snapped out of it. Mattie's head had to be saved before he could even think about his own needs. Spencer grabbed the head and pushed it into his open rucksack. The dogs growled loudly. He grabbed a nearby branch and jumped to his feet. The smaller dog lunged for him, but Spencer sideswiped the animal and rolled to safety.

The larger dog jumped on top of him, it's jaws bearing down on his neck. Spencer was able to get the branch into the dog's mouth before it made contact. His rucksack had rolled away from him. Spencer used all his strength to keep the larger dog away from his neck.

It was about that moment that Spencer spotted the smaller dog edging closer to the other side of his head. He had no more free arms to protect himself from another attack. It looked like this was the end. Spencer had come so close, but yet so far from achieving his goal.

Chapter Twenty Six

"It was here twenty minutes ago", Mr Wilson glanced around the small carpark that was out the back of his funeral home. His latest hearse, the pride and joy of his small fleet, was missing, "I parked it myself"

"Did you leave the keys in the ignition again dad?", Katie knew her father's daily routine well, and the bad habits that he kept repeating, no matter how many times he was told not to do them. One of which was leaving the keys, to any car, in the ignition.

"Only for a minute", pleaded Mr Wilson as he glanced around the carpark once more, hoping that the hearse would miraculously reappear out of thin air.

"Hello, I'd like to report a stolen vehicle", Katie was already on the phone to the local Garda station, "yes I can hold", she put the phone to her chest while she spoke to her father, "I'll sort this out. Will you go see is the bone rattler still working"

The bone rattler was one of the first hearses that Mr Wilson had ever owned. It was the ultimate work horse for the funeral home in its day, but now it had fallen into disrepair, and it most definitely earned its nickname. The suspension was shot and the engine wasn't tightly connected to its mounting anymore, so that led to the hearse shaking roughly as it was driven around. Katie had suggested scrapping it years ago, but Mr Wilson couldn't bare to see it destroyed. That's how it had ended up in the garage for the last seven years. Now it was the old car's time to shine. Hopefully.

Inside the funeral home, Dolly checked her watch as there was no sign of Ellis yet, "where is that sister of yours?", she tried to keep her voice low as Father Michael said a few prayers before they headed to the church.

Father Michael was an elderly man who walked with a bit of a limp. No one knew how he had come to walk like that. Some said he was kneecapped during the Troubles, while others reckoned he just had a bad fall. Either way, the old man wasn't able for this life anymore and probably could do with retiring to some rustic resting home in the countryside.

"I've texted her ten times already", Sophie glanced at her phone discreetly, "she still hasn't replied yet"

Zara had been ease dropping on the mother and daughter conversation, "I can go out and ring her if you like?"

"That would be great dear", replied Dolly, even though the question wasn't direct at her.

Zara was used to this and just gave Sophie a knowing look before heading outside.

Frank copped a free feel as Zara past him by. For a blind man, he was extremely agile in when to suddenly need to raise his hands to deal with a phantom sneeze that never came.

On the opposite side of Mattie Jenkins's coffin sat Gary and Lucas. They were also having their own family crisis as three of their party were missing. Gary had texted his mother and brother several times already. He had gotten no reply until now, when his phone began to loudly play an old song that he had chosen for a ringtone. It echoed around the extremely quiet room.

Gary struggled to get the phone out of his jacket pocket, as Nirvana's smells like teen spirit got louder and louder with each second, "I'm really sorry about this", he finally pulled the phone from his pocket. His brother's name appeared on the screen. Gary was just about to answer it, when he noticed all the other faces in the room staring his way, leaving him with an awful dilemma on whether to answer the call or not.

"I'll take it outside for you", thankfully Lucas took the phone and rushed outside, leaving the priest to carry on with the service.

Outside, things weren't going much better as Mr Wilson pulled the dusty old hearse up to the main door.

Zara was still trying to ring Ellis, but soon her attention was drawn to the hearse as it clattered along with added noises that were more suited to a clown car at the circus, "what in god's name is this piece of shit?"

Mr Wilson tried to look proud of his old vehicle as he stood next to the driver's door, furiously rubbing off the bad words that were written in dirt on the side, "it's a classic. They don't make cars like this anymore"

"I can see why", Zara fired back as she glanced around the carpark for the better looking hearse that she had seen the day before, "where's the other one gone?"

"At another funeral", Mr Wilson lied, even though there was a Garda car parked near the reception door. Thankfully Katie was dealing with that. He was too embarrassed to admit his mistake.

Lucas took a message for Gary. Marcus and his mother were running a bit late, and they were gonna meet them at the church. Lucas found it a little strange, but figured it wasn't his place to say anything on the matter. He was way more interested in the hearse that had just pulled up beside him, and the heated conversation that the young woman nearby was having with the funeral director. To be fair, the car was a heap of junk and deserved to be scrapped, rather than still be in use.

"Doesn't sound the best", Lucas couldn't help pointing out the obvious, "do you want me to take a look?"

Mr Wilson looked him up and down. Lucas definitely didn't look like a mechanic in his fancy suit with its pink silk shirt and matching tie, "do you know much about cars?"

"My father was a mechanic", Lucas replied, "taught me everything I know"

"Can't make it sound any worse", Zara added.

Mr Wilson soon relented and opened the bonnet.

By the time the prayers had been all said and Katie was wheeling Mattie's coffin out to the hearse, followed by the grieving family, they were met with the sight of Zara, Lucas and Mr Wilson with their heads stuck in low above the engine of the hearse. Lucas's hand were covered with oil, while Zara cleaned a filter with a dirty cloth.

Frank was wondering why everyone had stopped, but still used the opportunity to sneakily grab the ass in front of him, "oh, sorry about that my dear. It's hard to be blind at my vintage age"

"That's my ass you stupid asshole", Cilla whispered discreetly in her husband's ear while trying to stay smiling, "and if you make a fucking show of me today, I'll move around all the furniture at home again and watch you fall on your ass for the next week. Have you got that?"

"Loud and clear dear", Frank knew better than to cross his wife. She turned a blind eye to his wandering hands, and he said nothing about her many affairs. Easy to make a marriage work when you ignore each other's sexually deviant behaviour.

Dolly wanted to explode when she seen the state of the hearse, but she didn't let herself down and bottled the rage that was growing inside her. There was a lot of important eyes on her that day and she wasn't gonna let herself down, "is there a problem?", Dolly really wanted to batter Mr Wilson's head off the bonnet of the car, but she held herself together.

"No problem", Lucas answered for Mr Wilson, as he put the filter back were it belonged and closed the bonnet, "just giving it a fine tuning"

Thankfully Katie tried to get the show back on the road and began to load Mattie's coffin into the back of the hearse.

It was while all this was going on, that Lucas pulled Mr Wilson aside for a quiet word, "your hearse is absolutely fucked"

"Is that your professional opinion?", Zara was still standing close to them and couldn't help giving a sarcastic reply.

"My new hearse was robbed only a half hour ago", Mr Wilson couldn't see the point in trying to cover it up anymore, "this is all we have at such short notice"

"The car is a death trap", Lucas replied, "it shouldn't even be on the road, let alone being used for a funeral"

"It's only for today and I'll have something sorted by tomorrow. Please, it'll be okay", Mr Wilson was fearful that a refund was on the cards and he couldn't afford to be losing money right now.

Zara felt sorry for the old man and tried to stick up for him, "I'm sure it'll be fine for the next few hours"

Mr Wilson was delighted with the moral support and nodded in agreement.

Lucas felt there was no point in saying any more on the subject, "fine then", and headed back to give Gary some much needed moral support, before everyone got into their cars and followed the smokey old hearse on the three mile journey to the church.

Chapter Twenty Seven

Rory and Bernard had decided to skip the funeral home
that morning and headed straight for the church. They
got a taxi in the hope that today was the start of another
good drinking session in Mattie's name. They'd both
gotten their good suits out and were ready for anything.
Bernard stinking of cheap aftershave and Rory of
mouthwash.

As they passed a row of parked cars, a drunken homeless
man stretched out his hand, "can you give us a hand
mate?", he asked in a deep south east accent.

Bernard pretended to check his pockets, "sorry mate, no
change on me"

"I don't want your feckin money you stupid asshole", the
homeless man was getting more irritable, "I just need a
hand up"

Rory grabbed the homeless man's hand and pulled him
up to his feet. He spotted a guitar case on the ground
nearby, "is this yours as well?", and picked it up for
closer examination.

The homeless man snatched it away like a bold child,
"nobody else gets to hold my Betsy"

"Fine then", Rory was starting to regret helping the
homeless man up, but the more he studied the
overweight hairy reddened face, something seemed

strangely familiar about him. He just couldn't be sure why.

"Where's this church?", the homeless man glanced around, as he held onto the edge of a parked car with his free hand.

"Right there you blind fuck", Bernard pointed to a large building that was only a hundred feet down the road.

"Ah, perfect", the homeless man fixed his few straggled hairs and tried to walk, but he stumbled into Rory just as quickly, "do you mind giving me a hand son?. These legs of mine are a curse on me"

"And the fucking drink by the looks of it", Bernard mumbled under his breath.

They walked a few feet until the homeless man suddenly stopped, pulled out a key and pressed a button on it, that made the car from where they had found him on the ground, bleep, "you can't be too careful these days", he announced to anyone listening, before heading on towards the church, with the help of Rory.

The church itself was a fairly old fashioned building that was in dire need of repair and cleaning. There was scaffolding on all sides and two large twenty foot skips sitting close to the side of the building. There was some rather rough looking kids pulling copper from between the folds of tiles and brick. Seemed safer just to ignore them and get on with your own business.

Bernard spotted two fine looking women outside the main door of the church, smoking. Had to be a mother and daughter, but he would play the sisters routine to keep the mother sweet. They both wore skimpy black dresses and totally non matching red footwear. Bernard figured that if all went well, he'd get to fuck the daughter and Rory could take on the mother. They just had to play their cards right.

But before Bernard got a chance to work his magic, the older woman turned to see them and her face lit up, "oh my good god, it's the Mushy fucking Pea", she ran towards the not so homeless man and hugged him tightly, "I'm such a big fan and I've got all your albums including that stuff you did in the nineties with all those young people"

"Always nice to meet a fan", the Mushy Pea seemed to have suddenly grown a third leg and was rubbing it off the woman's bare thigh like a horny old dog, "maybe you'd like to join me later and we could make sweet music in the back of my car. What's your name, my beautiful queen?"

"Ellen", the excited woman replied, as her face drew closer to his, "always wanted to get it on with a celebrity"

"Looks like today is your lucky day", the Mushy Pea replied as he moved in for a kiss.

"For god sake mam", Jamie was getting sick of her mother's antics. Ellen had already flirted with the young priest who was definitely more in Jamie's age group, "can you not go one fucking day without making a show of us"

Bernard didn't want to waste the opportunity of making himself known and pushed past Rory to make his introduction to the young woman, "hi, I'm Bernard and you are?"

"Gonna be sick if another dirty old fucker hits on me today", Jamie had enough of pensioners and the near dead trying to look down her top while they made idle conversation on their way into the church.

But Jamie had caught the eye of the Mushy Pea as well, and he brushed Ellen aside and marched forward, "and who is this fine looking young thing here?. You've got a face like an angel, the figure of an hour glass and legs that could stop traffic. I just wanna ask you one thing. When do they open?"

"You cheeky bast….."

It was at that moment that Father Jessop, the young apprentice priest, made an appearance. Jamie was mad into him something shocking. She'd already flirted with him. But he seemed more scared of her than anything. Thankfully Jamie liked a challenge and decided to pursue it further. That meant being a good little girl and not verbally abusing pensioners, whether they deserved it or not.

"Hi Father Jessop", Jamie turned on the charm as her fanny got wet from just smelling his expensive aftershave, "need help with anything?"

Father Jessop was visibly scared looking, "I'm okay thanks", he turned to the Mushy Pea, "I see our celebrity has shown up"

The Mushy Pea fixed his hair and attempted to stand up more straight than he already was, "are you trying to insinuate that I wasn't going to show up?"

"Nothing like that", Father Jessop started to slowly shrink away towards the door of the church, "just glad you could make it"

But the Mushy pea wasn't letting it lie and carried on, "I'm a global superstar"

"Was, by the looks of it", Bernard whispered to Rory, who nodded in agreement.

"I've had thousands of young virginal women throwing their bodies at me", the Mushy Pea gestured towards Jamie as some kind of example.

"I doubt that", Jamie mumbled under her breath, but she did like being mistaken for a virgin.

"So I don't have to take shite off you, a jumped up little priest with a napoleon complex", the Mushy Pea fixed his suit jacket and stormed towards the fearful young man.

Jamie jumped in the way, her cleavage heaving with the sudden movement, drawing all male eyes in that direction, "leave him the fuck alone. Father Jessop is a sweet man who doesn't need bullying pricks like you annoying him. Now go get set up and less mouthing out of you"

The Mushy Pea threw her a leering smile, "you'd definitely be my catch of the day, if I'm a little more careful about how I sink my hook", and with those words, he marched past Father Jessop, into the darkness of the church, followed by an excited Ellen who kept asking him questions about his songs.

Jamie seen this as the perfect opportunity to turn on the charm with the good looking priest, "I don't like to see bullies getting their way. So where were we?. Like I was asking you earlier, is all this celibate stuff real?"

Rory and Bernard had heard enough and headed over to a nearby wall for a smoke. Both of their eyes still trained on the attractive young woman's red leather boots covered legs. Both of them wishing they were twenty years younger, but neither vocalising it.

Chapter Twenty Eight

"How are you holding up?", Zara noticed that her fiancé was struggling to bottle her emotions and the odd tear was running down Sophie's face.

"I'm okay thanks", Sophie squeezed Zara's hand tightly, "as long as I have you by my side"

"And you'll always will", Zara smiled.

"Nothing's forever", Dolly blurted out as she stared out the window of the limo at the buildings they passed by, "look at my poor Mattie. Thought he'd never leave me, and look where we're heading now"

"Some of us didn't get so lucky", Cilla mumbled under her breath.

"What's that?", asked Frank. But he didn't get an answer from his wife.

"Am I still bringing up one of the gifts Dolly?", Zara had been nervous about taking such a big role in the proceedings, but she was also honoured to be asked.

"I'd like you to carry the bottle of Sambuca. That was always Mattie's favourite little tipple when he wanted to get seven sheets to the wind"

"What's Sambuca?", Frank muttered.

"It's a drink", Cilla checked her makeup for the tenth time in a small mirror she always carried in her handbag, "that's not your concern for now. You need to be careful when you're bringing that ship up to the altar. You better stay close to me and Zara, and not go wandering off while we all walk up the aisle together"

"And what are you carrying?", Frank had a pretty short attention span.

"I'm carrying the candle", Cilla's voice was growing more irritable.

"And what does that signify?"

"Nothing, it's a fucking candle"

"And what about the ship then?"

It was only then that Cilla realised that she didn't actually know what the ship represented and turned to her sister for help.

Dolly was quick to answer, "Mattie always loved the sea and had fond memories of the fishing boats that he once worked on as a teenager. The boat you'll be carrying Frank, was made by Mattie himself. He used to love all those model kit things. I have a room full of them at home"

The only person that still had concerns about the plan was Zara. She figured that Frank's wandering hands might become a problem on the walk up the aisle. She just prayed that the model ship was big enough to require the use of both his hands.

Three cars back, Gary was trying to stay in the procession with all the other slow moving traffic. He would have happily just put the foot down and make short time to the church. Gary was also trying to ward off the many mental images of the recent sexual encounter he'd had with Lucas, that kept running through his head.

Lucas was still trying to make conversation ever since they'd left the funeral home, "what do you think happened to your mother and Marcus?"

"I've no idea. Didn't bother asking", Gary was feeling more and more uncomfortable about being seen in the presence of Lucas. His old friend was obviously gay to anyone that seen or met him. That was impacting on his own macho image and Gary wasn't liking that one bit.

"You've been pretty off with me since we left the hotel", Lucas wasn't stupid and had been in this position before, many times.

"I'm not being off with you", Gary lied, "it's just a pretty stressful day and I'm trying to get through it. Please stop thinking into things"

"You're embarrassed to be seen with me", Lucas stared out the windscreen as he spoke, "that's okay, I'm used to it. Austin was the same at the start"

"I'm not embarrassed, and what's this got to do with your boyfriend?", Gary was still struggling with his own emotions, and the last thing he needed right now, was to be compared to Lucas's boyfriend.

"Nothing, I was just saying that it's okay to feel a little weird after what we did. It's only natural. Austin was like that with me at the start, but he soon got over it"

Gary suddenly pulled the car out of the procession and parked it up against the kerb while all the other cars past them by.

Lucas was confused, "why did you do that?. We're gonna be late if you park here"

"I don't give a shit about being late", Gary couldn't even look at his old friend as he spoke, "what happened earlier on and last night, was a once off. We had sex and that was that. There's nothing gonna happen between us. We're not gonna end up in some wonderful relationship were everything works out perfectly. At the end of the day I'm into women. Doesn't matter how many times you lure me into bed with alcohol or my grief. Nothing is gonna change that, and the sooner you can get over that shit, the sooner we can go back to being friends"

Lucas tried not to laugh at the absurdity of his friend's mini rant. It was just like old times again. They may have both matured, but some divides just never changed, "I thought we'd be over all this stuff by now. That we could finally be on a level playing field for once"

"Well you were mistaken", Gary snapped back as he lit up a cigarette.

"That I was", Lucas opened the car door, "I'm gonna head off now. Don't wanna make this day any more stressful on you"

"That would be a big fucking help", Gary hated himself for saying those words, but he wasn't one to backtrack.

"Okay then, see you around sometime", Lucas slowly got out of the car, still hoping that his old friend would change his mind.

"I highly doubt our paths will cross again", Gary stared straight ahead as he firmly bottled down his emotions.

Lucas shut the door behind him and stepped away from the car. Gary then pulled back out into heavy traffic and sped off down the road, much to the annoyance of other road users who loudly beeped their frustrations.

Meanwhile, the limo had pulled into the front courtyard area of the church.

Dolly had spotted the many photographers standing around the high metal railings that circled the church boundary walls, "can't believe the media is out for this today"

"It's not for us mam", Sophie handed Dolly her mobile phone and showed her the footage of Marcus having a threesome, "looks like my half brother has started a little scandal for himself while back home"

"Oh my", as Dolly watched the video, she couldn't help wonder what happened to some of the footage that Trevor had taken of them during one of their more energetic love making sessions. He said it was all deleted, but Dolly still had her doubts.

The noisy hearse parked in front of the door of the church and the crowds started to gather around to watch as the coffin was taken out of the back by Katie and Mr Wilson. Sophie, Dolly and the rest of their group watched on from the sidelines.

Gary was standing near them. He was starting to regret driving away Lucas. Now he was all alone in a crowd full of people. Thankfully a familiar face pushed through the crowd and hugged him tightly.

It was Aisling, "you look like a lost lamb, all here on your own"

Gary hugged her longer than usual, "was afraid you weren't coming"

"Wouldn't dare miss this", Aisling was trying not to cry, "I know you were never that close to your father, but he was always nice to me and the kids, especially after we broke up. I can never forget his kindness"

Gary was aware that Aisling had met his father several times over the years, but it was starting to sound like, that they had met up a lot more after their divorce, "what kindness?"

"We were just finished. You hadn't the money to support me and the kids. I didn't wanna be putting extra pressure on you, because I knew your business wasn't doing that well, so Mattie offered to help pay the mortgage for a while. He didn't want you to know about it. Said you would be angry", Aisling felt guilty for keeping that information from her ex husband for all these years, but she couldn't hide the truth any longer.

But it wasn't as guilty as Gary was feeling right now, since he had lied about how well his business was doing at the time, just to get out of paying too much to his ex wife and kids, "I didn't know"

"I know you didn't. Don't worry about it. That's all in the past now", Aisling rubbed his stubbly cheek.

Inside the church, Ellen had been on lookout duty, and as soon as she seen the hearse pull up, she ran up the aisle to tell the Mushy Pea to start playing. Unfortunately she wasn't great at moving fast in high heels and fell flat on her face.

Her daughter, Jamie, finally looked away from flirting with Father Jessop, "you okay mam?"

Ellen looked up from the floor, "the hearse is here"

"THE HEARSE IS HERE", Jamie shouted over to the Mushy Pea.

The Mushy Pea was taking another shot of whiskey from his silver flask, that he had robbed many decades ago off Willy Nelson at a charity concert in the states, "I'm fucking ready", he strummed a few chords on his guitar, "Betsy is ready and all"

"Then fucking play", Jamie fired back.

The Mushy Pea broke into one of his old ballads about a haystack where he lost his virginity. Wasn't the most suitable song for a funeral, but at least he was slurring the words that much that no one could make out the risqué lyrics.

The coffin was wheeled into the church by Katie and her father, followed by Dolly and her family. People were filing in the side doors and rushing to get good seats near the front of the church. Gary followed the Dolly entourage with Aisling thankfully by his side. He couldn't believe he was trapped at his father's funeral, where he definitely didn't want to be, and there was no sign of his mother and brother. This was quickly turning into a nightmare.

As Sophie neared the front row, she caught sight of Ellis standing in the pew with another woman dressed all in black. She moved in beside her, followed by Zara, Frank, Cilla and finally her mother Dolly.

"Where the hell were you all morning?", Sophie whispered.

"I've had a lot to deal with so please don't get on my case", Ellis didn't even try to meet her sister's firm gaze. Instead, she just stayed staring at Father Michael, as he hobbled up the steps to the altar.

"What could be more important today than burying our father?", Sophie fired back while still trying to figure out who was on the far side of her sister, "who's that next to you?"

Ellis kept her eyes focused on the altar, "it's Steven, but he now wants to be called Stephanie"

Sophie was lost for words at first, as she studied the heavily made up side features of the other woman's face. Indeed she had a striking jaw line, just like Ellis's boyfriend Steven had, but no way this could be happening. Not today, not never.

"You're shitting me", Sophie's voice was starting to raise a little.

"What's going on?", asked Zara.

"That's Steven", Sophie whispered, while nodding over at the heavily made up woman.

"Fuck off", was all that sprouted out of Zara's mouth, which she covered as soon as the words slipped out.

"Can we talk about this later", Ellis never wanted to talk about it again. She still couldn't cope with it herself. She was just going through the motions for now, to keep Steven happy. He'd been proud of himself that morning when he made the admission, but it had all moved too quickly from that moment. There was even talk of them trying sex that night while he was still done up. Ellis was dreading the thought of it.

The funeral started off well enough. That was until Father Michael started to welcome everyone to the service over the microphone, which drowned out the Mushy Pea and his singing. He was only half way through his twelve minute ballad about losing his virginity in a haystack, and he was well known for being a tad particular about finishing off a song properly, when once started.

The Mushy Pea got up from his seat in the corner and smashed the body of his guitar off the ground without warning, before waving the damaged wooden neck around with the strings still hanging off, "you can't silence talent", he slurred loudly, before marching out of the church.

Ellen was glad that she wanked him off before the service. At least she had something to boast about to the girls when she got home.

Soon it was time for the offerings. Zara led the way out of the front pew and down to the centre of the church, were there was a small table with the offerings on it. Cilla had been following closely behind, along with Frank.

They stood waiting patiently to be called up by the priest, but Frank was more concerned about his wig. A gust of wind earlier had tossed it around, and he hated the thought of people not seeing him at his finest, so he searched around the table with his hands for some holy water. Frank reckoned there had to be some around here somewhere.

Finally his fingers made contact with a glass bottle and he liberally poured a good amount onto his hands. A lot of it ended up splashing all over the small table and the other gifts, but Frank didn't care as he rubbed it over the stray hairs on his wig and patted them down. The water smelt funny. Familiar, but still too far out of reach to place.

Soon the priest called them up. Zara grabbed the bottle of Sambuca, Frank picked up the model boat, and Cilla took the large candle.

It was all going well as the three of them reached the altar. That was until the main doors of the church was kicked open, and in stormed a very dirty and bloody Spencer Cruise. His clothes were badly torn and whole sections were missing from his pants. There was teeth marks covering his arms and legs. But Spencer wasn't bothered by all his newly acquired injuries as he marched up the aisle of the church.

Frank wasn't sure what was going on and turned to his wife, "what's happening?", it was then that he smelt the burning.

Unfortunately the candle that Cilla was holding had ignited the Sambuca that had been splashed onto the model boat, and it went up in flames in Frank's hands. That was the least of his problems as his wig caught fire as well. He threw the boat away and tried to put out the ever growing flames that sprung up from his wig. Cilla tried in vein to put them out as well, but the only course of action left open to her was to whip off Frank's wig before beating it off the steps of the altar.

Zara stood nearby, watching the chaos of it all and started taking swigs from the bottle of Sambuca.

Bernard had been watching on, a few rows from the front, as the small burning ship ended up in the baptismal font. He quickly nudged Rory, "it looks like a mini Viking funeral"

Spencer arrived at the coffin and turned to face the crowd, "no friend of mine is gonna be buried incomplete", and with that, he opened the rucksack he was carrying, pulled out the severed rotting head of Mattie Jenkins and held it aloft for all to see.

Silence fell over the whole church for a few moments as the congregation took in the horror of it all. It was pretty obvious to everyone in the first ten rows that the head was missing a lot of skin and one eyeball.

Unfortunately poor Father Michael found the stress of it all, was getting too much for him, and he collapsed into the arms of Father Jessop. A number of people started to vomit loudly in their seats, including Cilla and Aisling. Zara took another much needed swig of the Sambuca.

Jamie nudged her mother Ellen and declared, "best funeral, ever"

Chapter Twenty Nine

Things had been going from literally shit to worse for Marcus. After the unwanted wash in raw sewage, the three of them had to strip down to their underwear before the taxi driver would let them back in his car. Thankfully the guy had some blankets in the booth which he handed out to the dirty trio. Marcus had tipped him generously when they arrived back to the hotel. They then had to run through the lobby, drawing many uneasy glances from fellow guests and staff. Their faces still brown streaked and their hair battered down firmly like a day old cowpat.

Unfortunately the long showers hadn't gotten rid of the smell fully. Each one has sprayed themselves with a liberal amount of body spray and perfume. Thankfully Margaret had another dark outfit, but Carla was now stuck in blue jeans and a baggy red T-shirt, while Marcus had to wear white pants with a black denim jacket. It most definitely wasn't good funeral attire.

They then had to dodge the paparazzi on the way out of the hotel. Carla and Marcus with their shades on, running for the nearest taxi. Margaret stopped for a few photos until one of the reporters asked her about her son's sex tape. Margaret had heard him wrong and thought they were offering her to make one, so she called the reporter a "dirty little bastard", and punched him in the face, before jumping in the taxi.

They arrived at the church to find an ambulance outside the main door, along with a Garda car. There was no sign of Gary or any of Margaret's relatives or friends. Just Dolly standing against the wall smoking, while her twin daughters tried to console her.

"What's going on here?", Margaret asked her old enemy, "did we miss the funeral?. Can't be over already?"

"All you missed was a total disaster", Dolly pulled hard on her cigarette as Ellis tried to console her, "but I suppose that would suit your lot down to the ground"

"Please mam", Ellis pleaded, "we don't need anymore hassle today. Please just try and be civil for everyone's sake"

Sophie stepped forward and explained how Mattie had shown up with the head and Father Michael had gotten such a shock that he had a serious heart attack and was now in the ambulance that was pulling out of the car park, "we don't even know if the funeral can still go ahead today"

"At least he'll be buried whole", was all Margaret could say on the subject.

"Do you know where my brother Gary is?", asked Marcus to anyone that might have the answer.

Zara pointed towards a pub over the road, "most of the people from the church went over there, while they're waiting to see if there's still gonna be a funeral"

"Thanks", Marcus turned to his mother, "are you coming over the pub mam?"

"Can I talk to you in private?", Dolly asked Margaret. She had a lot to get off her chest, and now seemed the perfect moment to do it.

"Okay then", Margaret turned to Marcus, "I'll catch you up"

The group wandered off across the road, leaving the two women alone beside the wall of the church. Both of them smoking wildly at the tips of their cigarettes.

"Rang my solicitor this morning", Dolly announced.

"Good for you", Margaret fired back.

"He looked into that thing you said to me earlier. Turns out you weren't lying"

"I could have told you that"

"So he was kind of married to both of us"

"Looks that way"

"Why did he not tell me the truth?"

Margaret thought about that question for a bit, "probably fear if you ask me. He let it go on so long that there didn't seem to be a way back from it. Better to just keep it quiet and hope it didn't come. But don't be worrying. I'm not after your many millions or businesses. I'll sign what you want. Anything to protect your little family"

"Why would you do that for me?", Dolly was totally confused, "you've got nothing"

"Don't remind me", Margaret joked back, "just get your solicitor to draw up whatever you need to protect your kids inheritance, and I'll sign away any rights I have to Mattie's money. Can't say fairer than that"

Dolly was still reeling from all this when a little Chinese woman shuffled up towards them. She was carrying a baby in her arms and was pushing a twin buggy with two more kids in it, "is this Mattie Jenkins funeral?", she asked in broken English.

"It is", replied Margaret, "and who might you be?"

"My name is Eu-Meh", the Chinese woman replied, "Eu-Meh Jenkins"

Margaret and Dolly froze on the spot. Both unsure on how to reply to that.

Over in the pub, Bernard was turning on the charm with mother and daughter, "so you two fine looking ladies are from Drogheda"

"That we are", Ellen sipped at her double whiskey and tried to ignore the sweaty stale smell that was coming off the hand she had recently wanked off the Mushy Pea with.

Jamie had pushed up her tits, to get the most out of her ample cleavage, that was on show. It had already gotten her two free drinks off the young barman, "born and bred"

"I wouldn't have taken you two for mother and daughter", Bernard tried to turn on the charm, "definitely more like sisters"

Jamie's face dropped, "so you're saying I look old and decrepit like my mother?"

"Fuck you, you little bitch", Ellen fired back angrily.

"Ladies, ladies", Bernard tried to calm the heated moment, "how about I get us all shots from the bar", and with that he hurried off to get more alcohol.

Ellen smiled at her daughter, "another dope who'll easily believe anything"

Jamie tapped her mother's glass with her own, "you gotta love a horny middle aged man with a boner.

They'll happily empty their wallets at the sniff of a bit of fanny"

"I'll drink to that", Ellen replied, before downing the last of her drink.

Spencer was at the bar, pouring his heart out to an uncaring Mushy Pea, "there was so many dicks on show that I didn't know where to look. My beautiful Michelle was just surrounded by them. Never seen her in such a light before. Thought she was my angel , my princess. Now that all seems like such a big fat lie", Spencer was starting to realise that his marriage was truly over.

"Have you got a number for her?", mumbled the Mushy Pea, before he knocked back another shot of Jameson whiskey.

Katie's father had suggested she take a break from all the chaos, as he and the guards sorted out this head business in the church. She had found a quiet spot at the busy bar and was now enjoying a double vodka and diet coke. Rory had spotted her arriving in and had made a discreet move to near her vicinity. He needed to claim his territory before someone else took the opportunity.

"I bet you don't normally see all that mad stuff at your usual funerals?", seemed like a good icebreaker.

"I'm more worried for my dad's reputation", Katie wasn't in her usual good humour, "this isn't the type of publicity he needs right now. Driving poor Mr Jenkins around in an old shitty hearse is bad enough, but the chaos happening in the church is gonna make headline news. Don't know how the media got there so fast"

"You can thank our local celebrity for that", Rory pulled out his phone and showed Katie the footage of Marcus getting it on with two women, "it's always the quiet ones you have to watch out for"

"Don't get why everyone feels the need to film stuff like that these days", Katie looked away from the phone and went back to her drink, "I'm not an all holier than though type of girl, but I do think there's a lot of things that happen between a man and a woman that doesn't need to be shared for all to see"

"Or two women in Marcus's case", Rory joked back.

"Exactly. You've got all these celebrities making homemade porn movies and then they leave them around for someone to get their hands on. Why leave yourself open to such things. Never made sense to me"

Rory felt the conversation was going on too downer of a buzz and tried to claw it back onto the happy tracks, "how do you normally unwind after a day like today?", he hoped she was gonna say candles, chilled wine and cuddling up on the couch.

"I go the gym and beat the living shit out of a boxing bag", a smile came to Katie's face as she spoke.

"Looks like we have the next Katie Taylor right here then", Rory complimented himself on a great chat up line, "would love to see you in action", total double meaning and his mind was already imagining them having wild sex on the floor of his van. An impossibility at best, since the van was overly filled with his work tools.

"I'm not that impressive to watch", Katie could barely move the heavy training bag with each punch she landed. That's why she preferred to go when the gym was a lot quieter.

"Please let me be the judge of that", Rory could feel his erection growing in his pants and quickly began to think of Margaret Thatcher, in the hope of making it go back down again. Thankfully it worked for now.

Meanwhile, Gary was still upset about the way he had treated Lucas earlier, and thankfully he had someone he trusted more than anyone, to vocalise it to. Unfortunately he was trying to do it in a roundabout way that didn't mention his homosexual tendencies. That wasn't working too well for him. He and Aisling had found a quiet table in the corner and she was now caressing his hand.

"I treated him pretty shitty today", Gary couldn't even look in Aisling's eyes. The first time he had been unfaithful to her, was with Lucas. Yes, she had forgiven him for all the extramarital affairs he had throughout their time together, but that one still might hurt her more than the rest. Aisling had always liked Lucas a lot, and might see this as some form of betrayal.

"You're just grieving", Aisling rubbed Gary's shoulder in a way that she knew helped ease his troubled mind, "he'll understand. You could catch up with him when all this is over, and apologise. You're both adults now. Youse don't have to drift apart again like you did as teenagers"

Gary didn't need further reminding of his teenage years with Lucas. When he wasn't balls deep in Aisling, it would be Lucas. He internally cursed himself for letting his newer friends rule his life with their values and hatred of poofs or faggots, as they liked to repeatedly call them. Even the jokes about his own sexuality had gotten too much for him at times. Being forced to prove his masculinity by fucking endless other women behind Aisling's back. Now she was only one of two people that had been here for him over the last few days, and he had driven away the other one. There was no fucking sign of the rest of his so called friends.

"Lucas coming back, stirred up a lot of things from my past that I'd much rather forget" Gary tried to work his way around the brutal truth.

"Don't worry, I know", Aisling whispered in his ear.

Gary stared into her big caring eyes, "you know what?"

"I know something happened between you and Lucas when we were younger. It's okay. It was a confusing time for us all back then. We experiment, we try things, and a lot of those things don't always work out. I turned a blind eye to whatever was happening back then because I liked Lucas a lot. To be honest, my biggest fear was that you were gonna leave me for him at one point. I loved you so much back then, that I was willing to ignore the obvious. It was hard to watch when you turned your back on him. He was the best friend you ever had"

Gary broke a weary smile and kissed her on the cheek, "you're my best friend. Pity it took me so long to see that. We're better as casual lovers, than husband and wife"

"Ain't that the truth", Aisling laughed, "but don't let your head hold you back from what your heart wants. If there's still something there between you and Lucas, then you should explore it"

"But he's in a relationship", Gary replied.

Aisling's face went solemn, "I was talking to Lucas's mother a few months back, and she was worried for her son. That American guy he's with is suppose to be hitting him. Not just a few smacks, but literally punching the fuck out of him. I was surprised to see him at the funeral home yesterday. Supposedly the guy has Lucas on a tight leash"

Gary could clearly remember the bruises on Lucas's arms. It finally all made sense to him. His old friend had probably took a big risk to make contact again, and he had just fired it back in Lucas's face. What a fool he had been.

Outside, Marcus and Carla had finally reached the front door of the pub without bumping into any paparazzi. They'd all been too busy reporting about the unexpected arrival of the severed head of Mattie.

Marcus glanced back at the chaos that was his father's funeral and thought, "madness, absolute madness"

"Look on the bright side", Carla announced cheerily.

"And may I ask what that might be?", Marcus definitely couldn't see one.

"Your father's name will never be forgotten for hundreds of years. His death, and the chaos of his funeral, will fill vast amounts of space on the internet. People will be looking it up long after you and me are dead. We'll be lucky if even our own grandkids will remember us in a hundred years time"

"I've got a load of films behind me now. I'll be remembered for those", Marcus wasn't sure why he was protesting his case.

Carla gave him a solemn look as she placed her hands on each of his shoulders, "thousands of films come out of

Hollywood every year. Yes, most of them are porn and another big chunk of them are student bullshit that's not gonna go anywhere, but there is a good ten percent that makes a nice dent with the critics and audience goers. You're in that category right now. But it's only a very small one percent of those that people will still be talking about in fifty years, and even less than that in a hundred. So my point is, we'll all be forgotten to the depths of time, but Mattie Jenkins name will live on forever. Now let's go get a drink. My mouth is dryer than a ninety year old nun's fanny after a trip to Egypt", Carla then marched into the pub.

Marcus was still trying to make sense of all that Carla said, but soon gave up and followed her inside. A strong drink was much needed right now.

Up in a quiet corner of the pub, Sophie, Ellis and Zara were watching on as Steven, or Stephanie as he wanted to be called now, joked and laughed with a large group of people, who thought he (she) was a friend of the twins. No one knew the truth about what was really going on, and Ellis was happy to leave it that way for now.

"At least he's happy", Zara tried to put a positive spin on things.

"I'm still struggling to accept it", Sophie couldn't believe how wrong she had been about Steven, even though she wasn't sure whether this was better or worse.

"Can we please not talk about this right now",
announced Ellis. She was still trying to hold in the tears.

"It's a bit hard not to sis", Sophie replied.

"I'm going the toilet", Ellis got up and grabbed her black
handbag off the table.

"That's my one", announced Zara.

Ellis studied the handbag in her hand and noticed that the
gold studding was different around the handles. She then
spotted her own bag on the floor and picked it up, "fuck,
I'm sorry about that", before handing the other bag back
to Zara.

"No worries", Zara replied.

Ellis disappeared off into the crowd. She needed time to
clear her head.

Sebastian and Marco appeared through the crowd and
they all took turns hugging and kissing each other,
before they all finally sat back down at the small table.
They made idle conversation for a bit, before Sebastian
offered to buy a round of drinks for the table. Sophie
offered to help him carry the drinks back from the bar,
but truthfully she wanted to ask him more about the
other night.

When they reached the bar and Sebastian had ordered the
drinks, Sophie took the opportunity to try and put her

mind at rest, "have you and Marco talked much since we all did that the other night?"

"Do you mean are we struggling with jealousy over the whole thing?", Sebastian seemed to laugh it off a little before answering his own question, "we both knew what we were getting into with you and Zara, so there was nothing to be jealous about. Hope it's the same for you two?"

"It's not jealousy", Sophie protested, "it's more like I have this feeling that we didn't all take part in what we had planned out. Do you know what I mean?"

Sebastian's face went somber, "but I thought you and Zara had come to an arrangement together over that!"

"Over what?", Sophie was now totally lost.

Sebastian leaned in a little closer, so that no one else could hear him, "Zara said you were okay with it"

"Okay with what?", Sophie was starting to lose her shit.

"With her not having sex with either me or Marco. She said that you both talked it through, and had decided at the last minute, that it would only be you who tried to get pregnant"

Sophie couldn't believe what she was hearing. Betrayed by the woman she loved. Tricked into having sex with two men, so that Zara could boast that the child was conceived naturally. This was a major kick to Sophie's ego, and a major dent in her love life. Possibly a thick jagged crack that could never be fixed or hidden. But today wasn't the time to deal with such things.

Sophie leaned in close to Sebastian's ear, "I knew nothing about any of that, but please do me a big favour and let's just keep that piece of information between us for now. Deal?"

"I can't believe she did that", protested Sebastian.

"Have we a deal?", Sophie repeated herself more firmly.

"Okay", Sebastian reluctantly agreed.

The barman finally came back with the drinks. Sophie grabbed two of them and headed back to the table. Leaving Sebastian alone to pay, and more time to think about whether he had done the right thing by telling Sophie.

Chapter Thirty

Over the road in the church, Dolly and Margaret had just sat through a rather long story by Eu-Meh Jenkins. The young Chinese woman was only twenty seven, but her life had been marred by tragedy on several occasions. Not even the voices of the guards talking to a nervous Father Jessop could distract the three women sitting in separate pews, close to the rear of the building. Eu-Meh and her kids at the back, Margaret in the middle and Dolly at the front.

Dolly was struggling the most out of the three of them, "so you're trying to say that my Mattie married you, and had three kids", she'd been told all the kids names, but Dolly hadn't a clue how to pronounce them properly, so why bother trying, "and he never told you that he was married already?"

"No", Eu-Meh was visibly nervous as she breast fed one of her twins, "Mattie said he had a divorce from you. That it was all legal", she looked down at the floor sadly, "why did he lie to me?"

"All men lie", Margaret added to the mix as she played with the older one of Eu-Meh's kids.

"Ain't that the fucking truth", Dolly really needed a drink right there and then, but answers were more important, "you said that he helped out your parents. In what way?"

Eu-Meh stared at the floor once more, "my father and mother came over here for a new life. They have no English, so it was up to me and my two sisters to do all the translating for them. Made us closer as a family. When we finally built up the money, we opened massage parlour in centre of Dublin"

"Is this the one that Mattie owns the building that it's in?", Dolly was starting to see where this was going.

"Yes", Eu-Meh was glad that she didn't have to explain that part, "he owned building that my parent's business was in. We were struggling to pay the rent, so Mattie started to get a lot of free massages and happy endings"

"What's a happy ending?", asked Dolly.

"It's when the masseuse wanks off the guy at the end, for a bit extra", Margaret proudly announced, "I used to make a fortune doing it to the pensioners in the local nursing home. They might be old and decrepit, but they still like to shoot their load. Only the odd one had a heart attack during it"

Dolly threw her eyes up in disbelief, "the name black widow suits you more and more", she then turned her attention back to Eu-Meh, "so my husband was getting sexual favours off you and your two sisters?"

"And my mother", Eu-Meh added.

"This gets better and better", Dolly wanted to scream, "let's try this again. My husband was getting sexual favours off you, your two sisters, and your mother"

"And sometimes my grandmother", Eu-Meh added.

"Whatever", Dolly didn't need that mental image, "so he was getting paid off in other ways by your family. That doesn't explain how you ended up marrying him and having three kids"

Eu-Meh stared at the floor once more, "he started to like me more than the other women in my family. Said I was beautiful and he wanted to protect me"

"Typical Mattie", Margaret announced.

Dolly nodded in agreement.

"Said that he could stop charging my family rent, if I agreed to be his wife. My parents said that I didn't have to humour him further just to keep my family safe. But Mattie wasn't the worst of the men that came to our business. He was sweet in a way, and I figured it was some form of security for my family. So I married him four years ago"

Margaret spotted a large flaw in all this, "but were you not suspicious that he wasn't staying with you all the time?"

Eu-Meh shrugged her shoulders, "Mattie was a busy man. Always flying around the world on business meetings. When he got time, he would stay in my bedroom, above the massage parlour"

"Wait", Dolly needed to hold up the story for a sec, "you're saying he left you living alone with your kids in a two bedroom flat above your business?", Dolly was aware of the layout of the place since she went to go view the building with Mattie before he bought it.

"No", Eu-Meh continued, "my parents and two sisters live there as well. Can't afford rent anywhere else in the city"

Dolly couldn't believe how much her recently deceased husband had dropped in her personal standards. She wished the floor would open up and swallow her whole. Came as a welcome distraction when Father Jessop appeared out of nowhere and tapped her on the shoulder.

"I've been talking to the guards about whether we can go ahead with the funeral. They said that as the wife, you can just formally identify the head in their company and we can move on with the service", there was sweat pumping down the young man's face. Father Jessop definitely wasn't good at dealing with stress.

Dolly got up out of her seat and fixed the creases out of her clothes, "looks like the shit slinging is gonna keep coming my way for a good bit longer", she stepped out of the end of the pew and followed Father Jessop up the church.

Eu-Meh stared down at the floor again, "so I was never married in the first place. Mattie lied to me"

"All men are liars. It's just how you surf over their bullshit, that matters", Margaret wanted to tell the young woman that she wasn't the only one that was lied to about a proper marriage, but she didn't want to let down Dolly, "at least you got three wonderful kids out of it"

Eu-Meh nodded in agreement, "yes, I can't complain about that. Just hope this doesn't mean my parent's business is in danger"

"I'm sure it'll be okay", Margaret had a strong fear that the young woman was right. There's no greater danger than a woman scorned, and Dolly had been well and truly fucked over by Mattie. Margaret just hoped that Dolly wouldn't take all her rage and hatred out on poor Eu-Meh and her family.

Chapter Thirty One

The funeral finally got back under way, a whole three and a half hours after Spencer had walked in with the severed head of Mattie. The ambulance was long gone with Father Michael, and Father Jessop was doing his best to fill in. He struggled his way through a hand written eulogy to Mattie Jenkins. Constantly making mistakes as he went. Didn't help that Father Jessop was dyslexic as well. Something he had hid from his friends, family and work colleagues for years.

Frank was back in his seat near the front of the church. Both of his hands now bandaged up and still wearing his badly charred wig. Seemed a better choice than going bald. His wife Cilla was trying to act like nothing was wrong. Smiling like a Cheshire Cat as the service carried on. Not the best look for the funeral of a family member.

Jamie was growing bored with the long drawn out process of sticking someone in the ground, and was now trying to get a glimpse of Marcus near the front of the church. She'd seen him over in the pub during the half time break, but she hadn't gotten a chance to talk to him.

Jamie elbowed her mother discreetly, as she tried to get a clear look at him through the mourners, "that Marcus fella is a total ride, and he might be able to get me into the movie business if I play my cards right", Jamie fixed her bulging cleavage, so that a little more of each tanned breast seeped out over the rim of her tight low cut top.

Ellen leaned in close to her daughter so that no one else could hear her, "he might be your fucking brother so don't even think about it"

"Oh yeah". Jamie had forgotten that slight flaw in another one of her damn fine plans, as she liked to call them.

The rest of the family were solemn and quiet as Father Jessop still struggled his way through the long eulogy, "Mattie Jenkins was a man of honour"

"What bullshit", Dolly mumbled under her breath.

"And a good father"

"To which fucking family?", Margaret whispered to Gary, who nodded in agreement.

"He had such a colourful long life over the years. He touched a vast amount of people in different ways", Father Jessop was starting to find the confidence in his words. He wasn't even finding the young Chinese family in the front row distracting anymore. But he was sure that he hadn't seen them earlier, "Mattie was a cock to most people he knew"

All the bowed heads looked up from where they sat, each one unsure if they had just heard that right or not.

It was only then that Father Jessop spotted his mistake as he studied the hand written text of Father Michael a little more carefully, "sorry, I meant to say that Mattie was a rock to most people he knew", he pushed on and hoped that by not lingering on his mistake, people might not notice it so much, "and that he touched a lot of people along the way", that didn't sound right and he studied the text again, until suddenly he blurted out, "hearts, he touched a lot of people's hearts. Thank god for that", he wiped his sweaty brow clean. Father Jessop wished he wasn't the centre of attention anymore.

It was then that the double doors at the back of the church sprung open and in marched Heavenly Celeste and Tory Summers. Both wearing short black dresses that barely covered their crotches. Their matching high heels were giving both women a good extra six inches to their height. Both had shades on with matching small jackets and hats. They looked like a sexy modern feminist take on the Blues Brothers. Chad walked behind them in an expensive suit, looking all the high end male model that he was.

Their heels clicked down the whole length of the church and everyone turned their heads to get a better look at the well known Hollywood starlet.

Marcus knew that walk from the noise alone and whipped his head around to get a better look, "oh no"

"Oh yes", Carla whispered in his ear.

Father Jessop wasn't that up to date for a young man in his twenties. He had never heard of Heavenly Celeste or her few songs, "can I help you?"

"I'm looking for my husband. Heard this was his father's funeral", Celeste took off her shades and glanced around the church, before spotting Marcus cowering among the mourners, "oh there he is, hi Marcus", she started waving wildly over the heads of the crowd.

"What is this shit now?", Dolly had recently swallowed a Valium and was trying to keep her blood pressure down. She really didn't need anymore shite today.

"That's Marcus's wife", Ellis whispered to her mother.

"Surprised she looks so happy", Sophie added, "especially after that video of him having a threesome with his assistant"

"Marcus, I don't care what happened between you and Carla", Celeste stood at the end of the front pew, "I guess you were just trying to release some steam after what happened with me, Tory and Chad", she gestured towards her friends, who smiled and waved like a happy couple on their wedding day.

"Last night was a drunken mistake", Marcus stood up in his seat.

"Thanks a bunch", Carla muttered under her breath.

"Unfortunately everyone now knows about it, including you", Marcus had a strong feeling that all the people around him knew what his hairy cock looked like, and Carla's ass for that matter, and what they looked like when they were repeatedly mashed together like two pieces of ill fitting Lego.

"Thought it was only me that had the dodgy and explicit videos online", Celeste smirked, "you've blown all that out of the water", she aimed a thumbs up at Carla, "great ass by the way Carla"

"Thanks Celeste", Carla returned the thumbs up gesture.

"I love you to bits Marcus", Celeste wasn't one to wear her heart on her sleeve in public, but getting her man back was more important than her image, "please can we sort things out?. I really wanna make this work"

"So do I", Marcus was shocked to see that Celeste was missing him more than he missed her. It boosted his confidence in their future to no end.

Dolly had heard enough and stood up to address the loving couple, "it's all great that you two are working through your problems, but can we please get on with burying my husband?"

"Dolly's right son", Margaret couldn't believe she was agreeing with the woman who stole her husband. But now definitely wasn't the time for romantic reconciliations, "the two of you can talk about it later"

"Are you my mother in law?", Celeste beamed from ear to ear.

"Yes love", Margaret replied, "now why don't you sit beside your husband and we'll talk later"

Celeste finally got the hint and gestured to her friends to take a seat, before rushing around to the far side of the front pew and squeezing in past Carla, who fully enjoyed the experience of having Celeste's firm ass stuck in her face, "heavenly is right", she said quietly under her breath.

Celeste hugged tightly into her husband and smiled with pride, "love you so much"

"Love you too", Marcus wasn't sure had they really worked through things, but it was nice to have Celeste back on his arm again. He did love her and she did him. Just a pity about the baggage that both of them carried.

Father Jessop felt it appropriate to start back into his eulogy. This time being much more careful before saying each word out loud. Still didn't stop him from making five more mistakes before he got to the end.

Chapter Thirty Two

The walk to the graveyard had been a gruelling one. The noisy hearse had started to spew out large clouds of white smoke from its exhaust pipe, choking the family members close to the front of the procession. Didn't do much for Cilla's growing breathing problems and she fell back into the crowd a little, in the hope of escaping the fumes.

"Why do we all walk to the graveyard?", Rory had been wondering that a while now. Ever since his grandfather had died at the ripe old age of a hundred and three. Someone had the stupid idea back then, that they should all walk the four miles to the graveyard from the church. Didn't help that it was during a rather bad fall of snow and the strongest of the men in attendance had to keep pushing the hearse on, every time it got its wheels stuck.

"Don't know", replied Bernard. "Maybe it goes back to before we all had cars. Everyone had no choice but walk back then"

"True", replied Rory, "and there was no real entertainment back then, so a day out at a funeral was probably like going the carnival to some people. My granny always loved a good funeral. That old biddy lived for them. Free sandwiches, tea and coffee, meeting people you hadn't seen in ages. She said it was just like a wedding, but cost you ten times less money to partake"

"Your granny was a wise woman"

"Oh that she was"

Mr Wilson was still struggling with the hearse's engine. He was doing everything in his power to keep the vehicle moving along at a steady speed, but the smoke was getting worse and the noises out of the engine were getting louder. He rang Katie who was walking in front of the hearse and hoped her phone was on silent, and that she had her earpiece in. He wasn't too happy with her listening to music while they worked, but now it came as a relief.

"Katie, I don't think this motor is gonna make it up the final hill to the cemetery", Mr Wilson studied the dials on the dashboard. They were steadily going into the red, one by one. One was for the temperature of the engine, but the rest he had no clue of their purpose.

"Just give it everything on the hill and don't worry too much about losing the people behind. Better to get to the top alone, rather than not get there at all", replied Katie, "Just give me fair warning so that I can get out of the way"

"No bother, will do", Mr Wilson prayed it wouldn't come to such drastic actions.

Behind the hearse, Margaret was now pushing the twin buggy with Eu-Meh's kids it in, while Eu-Meh carried her youngest in her arms. There was a lot of confused people wondering why this Chinese woman, that nobody knew, was now leading the funeral procession. This led to a lot of speculation and gossiping among the crowds of people. Unfortunately most of them were on the money with their guesses.

Gary was in a world of his own as Aisling hugged into his side. Marcus was also linked arm in arm with a smiling Celeste who just didn't seem to comprehend that she was at a funeral and not on a movie premiere's red carpet, as she smiled and waved at other people in the crowd.

Sophie was quietly fuming as she played over in her head what she was gonna say to Zara when she got a chance later on. She'd even started to dig her own long nails into the palms of her hands as a way of trying to control her negative emotions.

While Ellis just tried to ignore the fact that her boyfriend now wanted to be a woman at more family events, and that he was nowhere to be seen. Steven had been getting on so well with some of the older members of the group, that he chose to go in their car to the graveyard instead.

The only support Ellis had right now was her mother Dolly, who marched along behind the hearse proudly, never once showing any signs that this day was going to total shit and more. All she had to do was get her cheating husband in the ground and it would all be over. She'd only have to show her face at the afters for a bit and then she could go home and partake in some real heavy drinking. Maybe even invite Trevor over if no one else came back to the house with her. Dolly felt like being used and abused by the younger man right there and then. Felt only right after the shite day she had just experienced.

The hearse reached the bottom of the hill and Mr Wilson put the foot down and revved the engine loudly, sending out another cloud of smoke that enveloped everyone in the front three rows of mourners following behind. The engine clanked loudly, but Mr Wilson wasn't getting any more speed out of the hearse.

Katie glanced behind her to see a wall of smoke billowing up from behind the hearse, and thanked the lord that she hadn't agreed to drive that day.

Everyone was coughing and spluttering as they struggled for air. Even Dolly couldn't keep her perfect image any further and started to cough loudly.

The group of mourners started to fall back and soon left a good twenty foot gap between them and the hearse. Mr Wilson tried to go into a lower gear, but it clunked loudly as it fought off his actions with loud grinding noises that wasn't doing any favours for the engine.

"We're gonna end up pushing this piece of shite", moaned Gary.

"You can have the side with the exhaust", Marcus tried not to laugh, but unfortunately Celeste did, loudly and without any signs of trying to hide it.

Carla was following behind and threw her eyes up, "I need a drink", she muttered to herself.

The hearse finally reached the gates of the graveyard and everyone took a deep sigh of relief as the engine was knocked off and all the smoke started to disappear. Mr Wilson was nervous about facing the mourners behind the hearse, so Katie took over the proceedings and opened up the back. She positioned the six men that would be carrying the coffin. Putting the two smallest at the front, which was Marcus and Rory. In the middle was Marco and Frank. Cilla had insisted on her husband being part of the coffin carrying, even though he was legally blind and his two hands now looked like giant earbuds. At the back was Gary and Sebastian. The six of them tried to move as one. Like a giant fucked up human centipede. Didn't help that poor Frank kept stumbling over the edges of paths and grassy stumps in the ground.

As they walked through the old part of the graveyard, and were getting closer to the new section, everyone was getting a strong sensation in their nostrils, as if someone had farted. They all couldn't help from sly eyeing each other suspiciously.

Margaret felt that she should say something on the matter, "don't worry everybody, that's just the smell of the raw sewage that was spewed all over the field earlier"

"What raw sewage?", this was the first that Dolly had heard about any of this.

"They hit a pipe in Mattie's grave earlier and it spewed out all over the place", Margaret did the hand motions to describe a geyser, "so they had to move him to another part of the new graveyard"

Dolly couldn't believe she wasn't told about all this and wanted to verbally attack someone for this massive fuck up. But she'd come this far already through a heap of major fuck ups, so what was one more to add to the list, "fine then, let's just get this done"

The six men placed the coffin down beside the open grave and stood back so that the gravediggers could attach the straps through the handles and get them underneath and then back up the other side. Father Jessop was saying a few final prayers while trying not to catch the lustful eyes of Jamie, who had positioned herself right across from him. Dolly handed out roses to her two daughters and even gave the spare ones to Margaret and Eu-Meh. Then the men moved back in and took a hold of the straps once more and awaited instructions to lower the coffin down into the six foot deep hole.

Meanwhile, Mr Wilson was still outside the graveyard with the hearse. A lot of smoke was now pouring out of the engine and he was trying to explain on the phone to the woman from the AA, that he needed them to send out a tow truck to get the hearse out of there. But the woman on the phone was annoying pleasant and kept going through, what sounded like, a set list of questions for him to answer, and she didn't like to be interrupted, "I'm sorry sir, we have to go through my list before I know how best to help you"

Mr Wilson was starting to wish he was dead at that very moment.

Unfortunately he nearly got his wish as the engine of the hearse exploded like a poorly made Roman candle and sent him flying into a nearby hedge. The noise of the blast took the coffin bearers by surprise, as they were lowering the casket into the grave. Three of them lost their grip, and the other three found the straps running too quickly through their fingers.

The coffin smacked down hard into the grave. Frank unfortunately couldn't feel much with his bandaged hands, and the end of the strap got caught in the material and dragged him into the hole, along with the coffin.

Dolly didn't know what else to do, but throw her single rose in, on top of the coffin, "see ya Mattie. You've left me with more questions than answers", she then turned to the rest of the mourners and loudly announced, "you're all invited back to the function room in the Gresham hotel for a free bar and nibbles"

A big cheer went up and the crowd started to disperse from the graveside.

"Help me, please", moaned Frank as he struggled up to his feet in the grave.

Cilla threw her eyes up as she went back to get her husband out of the hole, "I'm fucking coming"

But Father Jessop had already ran to the old man's aid and was now assisting him out of the hole.

Chapter Thirty Three

Dolly had gone all out for the afters with a rather lavish display of finger food set out across a long table. There was even an ice sculptor of a younger and healthier looking Mattie, that was placed in the centre of the table. The bar was packed with dozens of people as they all tried to get a free drink.

Jamie and her mother Ellen had found the bottles of complimentary Prosecco. They had taken one each and were now necking it from the bottle. They then admired the ice sculptor while they loaded their handbags with sausage rolls and chicken tenders.

"He still wasn't much of a looker when he was younger", Jamie was struggling to see Mattie as any kind of a biological father to her.

"It's not always about looks", Ellen scolded her daughter.

"Well he was rich I suppose", Jamie replied.

"It's not about that either", Ellen thought about it a little bit more carefully, "but yes, it was nice that he could treat me right. But Mattie was more than that. He listened to me. I mean, really listened. And not that pillow talk shite, when fellas are too fucked after shooting their loads, so they just cuddle into you and listen on as you pour your heart out like a sad twat. That wasn't Mattie. He took an interest in me back then.

Made me feel special. You've never had that special moment with any of your male suitors. You'll never understand how the right man can make you feel"

Jamie glanced over at Father Jessop, who was talking to some of the mourners, "maybe I don't, but I think I've found the guy who might help me get there"

"Please don't shag the priest love", Ellen pleaded, "it doesn't get you anywhere in life. Besides, those men are married to god"

"Doesn't that make them gay?"

"Suppose it does in a way"

"Well I'm gonna find out for sure", Jamie threw her mother a cheeky smile before making a beeline for a very scared looking Father Jessop. He was like a rabbit in headlights, and Jamie was loving every minute of it.

Rory and Bernard had offered Katie along to the afters. She had graciously accepted. Seemed like a good idea since her father was thankfully okay after the exploding hearse, and there was no other work on that day.

Bernard had disappeared off in search of the hot looking woman in the red shoes, that he had met earlier in the church, giving Rory some much needed alone time with Katie. Both of them had two pints each, and had found a quiet corner of the large room to chat. They'd been getting on great, but Rory feared that the young woman was just seeing him as some friendly old man that probably reminded Katie of her grandfather, or another elderly relative. Rory was in two minds about approaching this question, but the added alcohol was helping to swing it one way more than the other.

"Can I ask you something?", Rory couldn't believe he was gonna go there.

Katie leaned on her hand and gazed into his eyes, "what would you like to ask me?"

"Do you see me as just some polite old guy, or something else?"

"What's the something else?"

"You know"

"Elaborate for me", a smile spread across Katie's beautiful face.

Rory bit the proverbial bullet, "would you ever go out with a guy like me?"

"Does this answer your question?", and with that, Katie leaned in and kissed Rory on the lips. Running her tongue around gently inside his mouth, before slowly pulling away again.

Rory was briefly lost for words, before he finally composed himself, "most definitely", he couldn't help from smiling like a Cheshire Cat, that got the whole damn truck full of cream.

Out in the adjoining corridor, Sophie had finally gotten a hold of Zara in private, and was trying to keep her temper at bay for now, "you fucked me over the other night. You didn't have sex with either of the guys. Why the fuck would you do that?. This was your plan for god sake", Sophie was now wishing that she had of laid off on the free vodkas and coke that day, as they were making her words slur a little, and her eyes were watering as well.

Zara struggled to look her fiancé in the eyes as she searched for an excuse, and when none could be found, she started trying to paint her reasons in a better light, "I like working Sophie. Haven't time to be taking months off work to give birth, and then raise a child for a few months. So I got cold feet in the end. Couldn't go through with it the other night. The fellas understood and accepted it. But I didn't think you'd be as reasonable, and I was right"

"This was your plan, god damn it, and I stupidly went along with it", Sophie wanted to kick herself for being such a fool, "I could have asked my mam for help with paying for artificial insemination, but you always said no. Had to be a natural conception to keep up with your family's high standards of what a normal couple, and potential parents should really be like. I bent over backwards for you for many years. Never seen this side of you in all that time. What the hell is going on with you Zara?"

"You wanted to go to your parents, once again, to bail us out of another problem. That's all your parents are to you most days. Let's be honest here. It's not actually your parents that bring in the money. Poor old Mattie was the bread winner of your family, and now he's been buried six feet under in an expensive wooden coffin with a load of fancy carrier bags inside", Zara straight away regretted her words, but it was too late to take them back, so just stood there stubbornly and owned them instead.

"Fucking bitch", was all Sophie could blurt out before running up a nearby set of stairs and out of view.

Zara called after her, and when that didn't work, she ran up the stairs as well.

Back in the function room, the Mushy Pea had somehow made his way to the afters, and had set up residence at the corner of the free bar. He had six different drinks in front of him, and he had another guitar case by his side. On the front of which was written, Betsy no. 347.

Spencer was next to him, drinking a pint of Guinness. The two men had formed a strange bond that day, and were now discussing their lives in detail. The Mushy Pea loved to talk and tell tales from his wild life, while others quietly listened in the background.

Bernard had finally caught up with the woman in the red shoes, and not long after, he and Ellen emerged from an unused cloakroom after they'd just tried things in there that most people wouldn't do in private.

Ellen was struggling to pull her skirt back down over the cheeks of her painful ass, "that's definitely not as much fun without lubrication"

"But spit is lubrication", Bernard protested, "god's lubrication at that"

"Give me KY jelly any day", Ellen muttered to herself as she headed back to the free bar for a much needed triple vodka and coke.

Zara was still searching the corridors for Sophie, when she finally turned a corner onto a small landing where there was a large window overlooking O'Connell street below. In front of which was a small table and two large leather armchairs. Sophie was sitting in one of them, crying.

Zara figured she had to apologise in some way, for what happened, and leaned down in front of her crying lover. She wiped the tears out of Sophie's eyes and fixed her few stray hairs, "it's gonna be okay. Everything is gonna be fine"

"It's not", protested Sophie, "it's all ruined now"

Zara did what she thought was the right thing to do in that situation, and planted a kiss on Sophie's lips. She lingered there for a few seconds before finally pulling away. Deep down hoping that her love could be felt through that one action.

"Sophie looked deep into her eyes, "Zara"

"Yes"

"Wrong sister"

"What?"

"She said, wrong sister", came Sophie's voice from behind her.

Zara swivelled her head around to see Sophie standing there, and only then realised that she had Ellis's face in her hands, which she let go of fairly quickly and stood up to protest her innocence to her fiancé, "I'm sorry. Never thought I'd get you two mixed up"

"None of that shit matters now Zara. We're finished, and that's that", Sophie didn't need much time to think things through. Her mind was made up.

"You can't just throw away what we have, just like that", Zara protested, "we're suppose to be having a baby and getting married"

"Well I ain't marrying you now", Sophie was finding her strength again, "and if I am pregnant, it'll be just me as the mother. You'll have nothing to do with this baby and that's final. Now get the hell out of my sight"

"Can we please talk this out in private?", Zara pleaded before turning to Ellis, "can you give me and your sister some time alone?"

"Ellis is going nowhere", Sophie walked around Zara and held her sister's hand, "she needs me right now. But I most definitely don't need you in my life anymore"

Zara finally got the hint that she had just destroyed a good thing, and it was too late to get it back again, so walked away from the twins. Never once looking back, for fear they'd see the tears in her eyes.

It was only then that Sophie let her own tears flow freely, as she sat in the opposite armchair to her sister.

Ellis leaned forward and rubbed her sister's knee, "you okay?"

"Not really", Sophie replied, "what about you?"

"Told Steven that I couldn't deal with Stephanie"

"How'd he take it?'

"Pretty good really", Ellis replied with another sniffle, "better than I'm fucking taking it. He's still downstairs getting on great with all our relatives"

"At least we don't have to entertain the pack of grumpy old bastards", Sophie wasn't a big fan of most of her mother's side of the family, and she knew Ellis shared the same views about them as well.

"Every cloud has a silver lining and all that", Ellis smiled.

Both sisters looked at each other, before breaking into laughter. It was just like old times again.

Marcus and Celeste were cuddled into each other at one of the circular tables that were dotted around the room. It barely dampened the mood that Tory and Chad was sitting next to them. Marcus so wanted his marriage to work, and so did Celeste. It was then she noticed a familiar face from her father's old record collection, sitting at the bar with a guitar next to him.

Celeste nudged Marcus and pointed over at the bar, "is that really the Mushy Pea?"

Marcus was surprised that she knew who it was. The Mushy Pea had been a pretty big irish celebrity in his day, but Marcus never would have guessed that his musical talents had reached outside the emerald isles, "supposedly he was playing in the church earlier. I missed it as well", he wasn't a fan so it didn't bother him that much.

"Do you think if I went over, would he sing something with me?. One of his classics, hopefully", Celeste was getting jittery at even the thought of singing with such a legend.

"No harm in asking", Marcus replied, "want me to come over with you?"

"No thanks", Celeste kissed Marcus on the lips as she climbed over him, "don't miss me when I'm gone"

"I'll try not to", Marcus joked back, but deep down he was gonna miss her. It felt great having Celeste back in his arms again. Just hopefully the sex thing wouldn't get in the way again.

But as Marcus watched Celeste march proudly through the crowd, he noticed all the other men looking her way. Celeste was always gonna be getting attention from many wanting eyes. He'd just have to get use to that, or move on altogether. Marcus just hoped it wouldn't come to that.

Celeste arrived at the bar next to the Mushy Pea, and only had to smile his way to get the old man's attention, "I'm such a big fan of your music. My dad brought me to a few of your shows in Nashville. He worships the ground you walk on. Mind if I get a photo?", Celeste didn't wait for the Mushy Pea to say yes, and turned to get a selfie with him. Celeste was so excited that she didn't even notice him looking down her top, to take in the most splendid view of her heaving cleavage. She posted the photo to her Instagram without checking it, and straight away a hundred plus followers liked it.

Unfortunately the Mushy pea had no idea who Celeste was, and brushed his thinning grey hair back with his free hand, "and what might your name be, beautiful young, attractive lady?", his eyes were taking in every curve of her sexy firm body. There was an erection growing in his pants and all.

Spencer nudged the Mushy Pea, "that's your one, Heavenly Celeste, that is", he turned to Celeste, "love your movies"

"Thanks very much", Celeste smiled back. She still loved getting compliments about her work. Even the hollow ones.

"So you're an actress", the Mushy Pea was slowly catching up with the conversation.

"And a singer", Celeste announced proudly, "and it would be a great honour for me if I could duet with you on one or two of your hit songs. Could that be possible?", she so hoped he'd say yes.

The Mushy Pea seemed to find a new strength from somewhere, as he leapt off the stool and grabbed Betsy from beside him, "we need a stage to perform, and there's a nice big one over there", he took off through the crowd as he made his way towards the large permanent wooden stage, that was risen a couple of feet off the ground and built into the wall of the large function room. It was normally used by wedding bands and the odd small musical act that didn't draw the largest of crowds, but refused to play a cheaper venue.

The Mushy Pea threw a stool up on stage, and his guitar. He then struggled to pull himself up over the lip of the stage. Thankfully Celeste gave his feet a bit of a push and the old man was up. Celeste took the easier way and went to the side of the stage and used the steps instead.

The Mushy Pea was already checking backstage, before finally coming back with two microphone stands, which he turned on and set up, "you'd be amazed at the shite that people leave lying around in places like this", he sat down on his stool and began to tune his guitar.

Celeste stayed standing. She could see Marcus through the crowd and gave him a little wave and a smile. She so wanted to make him proud that day. Prove that she could be just as much a part of his family and life, as he had been to her's the last few years. Marcus smiled and waved back. That gave Celeste a little boost that she didn't know she needed, but throughly accepted with much delight.

When the Mushy Pea was finally ready to play, he looked over at Celeste as his fingers gently plucked a few strings of Betsy the guitar, "what would you like to sing my dear?"

There was so many hits of the Mushy Pea that Celeste wanted to sing, but one song stood out more than most, "can we sing the old radiator in the wheelbarrow?", it was a fairly old hit song by the Mushy Pea, but Celeste always loved hearing it as a child.

"Your wish is my command", announced the Mushy pea and his fingers started to play. They moved lighting fast across the strings, unaffected by the drugs and alcohol in his system. Then he started to sing in that deep haunting voice that he was famous for, "ONCEEEE UP ON ME FARMMMM, THERE WAS AN OLD RAD I ATOR THAT SANGGGG. ITS NOISY BANGING YOU COULD HEARRRRR, AS THE CROWS NEARBY WOULD LANDDDD", the Mushy Pea nodded over at Celeste to start singing, and that she did. Flinging her voice into the next few lyrics about putting the radiator in a wheelbarrow and bringing it to town. All the mourners went quiet and listened. They all knew the song, some better than others, but when it finally hit the chorus, everyone was singing along loudly.

Everyone except Dolly, who couldn't believe her husband's funeral was turning into a mini concert for two celebrities. But she said nothing and backed away towards the exit. People were having fun and enjoying themselves. Seemed like no point in dragging down the mood of it all, by complaining. Mattie probably would have loved all this.

Suddenly a strong hand grabbed dolly's arm and dragged her out into the quiet adjoining corridor. Before she had time to protest, Dolly noticed it was her young lover Trevor. He liked to dish out his dominance over her from time to time. He had a fancy suit on, and the top few buttons of the shirt was open.

"Why are you doing this now?", Dolly protested as he pushed her up against a wall next to a small wooden counter, that was probably either used as a cloakroom, or for collecting money for shows in the adjoining function room. Part of the counter was raised up, and you could easily walk inside.

"Didn't want you forgetting about me anytime soon", Trevor had Dolly's arms pinned to the wall on either side of her, "I was getting bored up in your hotel room"

"I thought you were happy enough screwing that Tina one in my bed", Dolly wished she hadn't of mentioned it, as the image of the young attractive woman, bouncing up and down on Trevor's cock, came back to haunt her.

"Only so much tight little fanny that you can fuck, before you want the experience of an older woman, who knows what she's doing in the bedroom", Trevor's hand went up Dolly's dress and started to rub her pussy firmly, through the material of her underwear.

"Please stop that", Dolly pleaded. She knew that sooner or later he was gonna get his way, and that scared her more than anything. Trevor was well aware of her weak spots, and was more than willing to use them against her.

"You know you want this", Trevor kept staring down at Dolly, as his rough fingers rubbed firmly off her ever moistening pussy.

"Please just leave me alone", Dolly pleaded once more. This time her voice was starting to grow weaker and more timid.

"What did you say?", Trevor just kept on toying with his prey. He loved the control.

"She said leave her the fuck alone", Margaret had seen Dolly disappearing out into the corridor, and wanted to make sure that she was okay, but she honestly hadn't expected to find this.

Trevor turned around to face Margaret. The leering smile still on his face, "oh look, another sad old woman in need of a young cock. Sorry love, Dolly here has my busy schedule all took up, especially now since her husband is dead, so please fuck off back to whatever you were doing previously, and leave us alone", he turned back to a scared Dolly once more, "now, where were we?", he sneered.

But Margaret could see the fear in Dolly's eyes and wasn't gonna budge that easily, "I said leave her alone and fuck off, before I do something that I might regret"

Trevor got right up in Margaret's face, "what's an old battered and fat granny like yourself, gonna do to a young fella like me?"

Margaret kneed Trevor hard in the bollocks before grabbing him by the ears and smacking his shocked faces off her good knee. The blood pumped out of his nose like a busted bottle of ketchup. Trevor staggered back towards the opening of the counter. Margaret then landed a good punch on his jaw, that sent him falling to the floor unconscious.

Dolly was in shock at what just happened. Her eyes still staring down at Trevor's motionless body, "is he okay?"

Margaret grabbed Dolly's hand and guided her away from the area, "he'll be grand. Just needed a good knocking down a peg or two"

"What if he wakes up?", Dolly protested, "he's gonna be pissed", Trevor wasn't one to take even the lightest of verbal abuse, lying down. So he'd definitely be making a major scene after this shit.

"Don't worry", replied Margaret, "I'll set my Gary on him. That will teach the little prick a lesson"

When Dolly and Margaret entered the function room, the Mushy Pea and Celeste were just finishing off the last few lines of the old radiator in the wheelbarrow. But as soon as one song was finished, they went straight into another. People clapped loudly as the impromptu concert was gaining steam.

Margaret spotted Marcus, Carla and Aisling, sitting together watching the show, so she dragged Dolly over to where they were sitting, "anyone seen Gary?"

Aisling had hoped that no one would ask about her ex husband's whereabouts. She didn't want to give anything about his private life away, "he's gone to deal with something, and then he'll be right back Margaret"

Margaret couldn't believe her ears, "what could be more important than his father's funeral?"

Aisling chose her words carefully, while maintaining eye contact with her ex mother in law, "trust me Margaret, it's important"

Chapter Thirty Four

It had taken a while to get across town to Lucas's hotel, but still Gary wasn't in any great rush to run into the building when he finally arrived. No, he much preferred to sit outside in his car and practice what he was going to say to Lucas when they finally came face to face.

Kissing him seemed an easy option, but just not his thing. Gary prepared little speeches in his head, but each one hit a brick wall as he tried to second guess what Lucas would reply with. There was even a brief moment when Gary considered turning the car around and driving back to the afters without Lucas. Maybe not even go back to the afters at all, and save himself a lot of unnecessary hassle. In the end Gary decided to get it over and done with.

When Gary finally made it to Lucas's hotel room door, he could hear a lot of shouting coming from inside.

There was this tough American voice roaring, "THINK YOU CAN TREAT ME LIKE CRAP, DO YOU?", and that was followed by a loud slapping sound.

Gary could then hear Lucas pleading with the man to stop. It was pretty obvious that Austin had made an unexpected trip to Dublin.

Gary knocked the door, and that was followed by silence on the other side, until Austin finally ordered Lucas to open it. Gary tried to keep his cool as the door opened to reveal that Lucas had a pretty painful looking red mark around his right eye.

"Just came to apologise", Gary walked in past Lucas, before his friend had a chance to panic.

Gary finally got a look at Austin for the first time. The American was at least six and a half feet tall, built like John Cena and sporting a white T-shirt that was definitely two times too small for him. You only had to look at Austin, to know that he was a total prick, but Gary didn't show it, "and you must be Austin. Heard so much about you from Lucas here"

"Probably a lot of bullshit knowing Lucas", Austin threw Lucas a dirty look before turning back to Gary, "and I take it you're the fella that popped by man's anal cherry for the first time?. Nice to finally put a face to the dick", he laughed at his own poor attempt at humour.

"Are you two having a bit of a disagreement?", Gary might have relaxed his body language as he strolled around the room, but he was more than ready to kick off at brief notice.

"Lovers fight", Austin replied, "you should know that better than anyone, since the two of you fell out in the past as well", Austin pointed his accusing fingers at the two men.

Gary shrugged his shoulders, "real friends always fall out"

"But you two were more than that", Austin replied with a leering smile.

"But we were friends first and that's what should always come out on top", Gary replied while glancing occasionally at Lucas, "that meant more to me than anything physical that happened between me and Lucas. Was nice to get that bond back for awhile yesterday, and I fucked that up with my mouth"

"Well poor fucking you then", Austin turned off the niceties like a switch, and went into, angry bouncer at a Temple Bar nightclub, mode, "think it's time for you to go and leave me and Lucas to sort out our relationship problems"

"See you've been sorting out your problems on his face already", Gary gestured towards Lucas's damaged eye socket, "pretty nifty with your hands there. Makes me wonder would you be up for a real challenge?"

"Are you asking to fight me?", Austin pointed accusingly at Lucas, "over this little cum bucket"

"You're one of those big old pricks who throws around insults like they don't hurt anyone", Gary had a craving to light up a cigarette, but knew the situation wouldn't allow such luxuries, so took a piece of backup chewing gum from his pocket and stuck it in his mouth, "I'm a lot like you. Driving people away with my mouth, and alienating the ones I love, but there is one thing that helps me stand way above pricks like you"

"And what would that be?", Austin flexed his muscular chest, that seemed to have a life of its own as it moved and bulged like a large coiled up snake.

"I'm not a happy slappy fucker like you, who only gets handy with their fists, when their opposition is a lot weaker than them. You're all mouth and no balls mate. Bet there's nothing slapping off Lucas's ass when you're doing him doggy style"

Lucas couldn't help but let out a little laugh.

"You little fuck", roared Austin and he lunged himself at Lucas.

Lucas froze against the wall and waited for his lover to strike, but Gary swung a right hook and sent Austin flying into the old fashioned chest of drawers. Austin looked surprised at first, but soon got over it and launched himself at Gary, with a raised fist and his perfectly white teeth showing. Gary sidestepped it easily and rained down an elbow onto the American's back, which thankfully winded him. Gary then grabbed Austin's left arm and bent it back in a painful manner.

"Let me the fuck go", Austin roared as he tried to hide the pain he was now feeling.

"I will in a minute", Gary was enjoying the power of the moment, "just like letting big fucking assholes like yourself, know that you can't be going around beating up those that are weaker than you. You're not so tough now, are you?. All that muscle you're carrying is just overrated fat"

"Fuck you", Austin roared back.

"Grab your stuff", Gary ordered Lucas, before turning his attentions back to Austin, "we're out of her now, and you better never bother Lucas again, or I'll fucking make sure you regret that decision. Have we got an understanding?"

Austin didn't reply, so Gary applied more pressure to the American's arm, "have we an understanding?"

"Yeah, fucking yeah", Austin's face went bright red from the growing pain in his arm.

"Good lad", Gary noticed that Lucas was already standing in the doorway with his suitcase, "have you got everything?"

"I'm sorted", Lucas replied.

"Then let's get out of here", Gary let Austin's arm go and stormed out of the hotel room, shutting the door tightly behind him.

When the two men got back in Gary's cars, there was a long silence between them as both of them stared out the windscreen at nothing in particular. Both trying to make sense of what just happened.

"So where does this leave us now?", Lucas felt like he'd just broken away from the only life he knew. He could never go back to the apartment he shared with Austin. Lucas wouldn't be able to socialise with his friends anymore, because Austin would be there. Even his job seemed in crisis. But if he had to give up all that for a quiet, physical and verbal abuse free life, then it seemed like a small price to pay.

Gary was still mulling things over in his head. He was more concerned about the future, and what his friends would say if he shacked up with another man. It definitely would mean a major lifestyle change, "I don't know what's gonna happen between us. Maybe we could make it work. Who knows. But for now all that matters, is that you're away from that asshole, and that there's a free bar in the Gresham hotel for the rest of the day. So why don't we both go get rat arsed drunk and we'll worry about the future tomorrow. What do you think?"

"Sounds good to me", replied Lucas.

Chapter Thirty Five

Celeste was feeling pumped after her four song set with
the Mushy Pea. Unfortunately the old man had gotten
fairly tired and needed to retire back to the bar, where he
snorted a few lines of cocaine off a beer mat. He even
offered one to Spencer, who threw caution to the wind
and snorted it up quickly when no one was looking.

But Celeste wasn't put off by the lack of singing partner
or musical accompaniment. Turned out there was a
wedding in the next function room and the band wasn't
needed for at least three hours. All their equipment was
piled up backstage.

Celeste went looking for the band members, but was
taken aback to find out that they were all pensioners who
didn't know any of the songs she wanted to perform. So
Celeste gave them a thousand euros for the use of their
equipment, and to set it up on the stage, while she went
and pulled a band together.

First port of call was Tory and Chad. Both of them had
worked in the music industry over the years, as
musicians. Chad was up for it from the start, while Tory
was more concerned about breaking one of her acrylic
nails. She soon changed her mind when Celeste offered
to pay for her to go to a beauty parlour the following
day.

The elderly band members finally had the stage ready.
They then wandered off to the free bar and mingled with

the mourners. Celeste, Tory and Chad got up on stage and started to get ready to perform. Chad pulling off his jacket and unbuttoning his shirt, before taking that off as well, to reveal his strangely shiny, tanned washboard stomach.

Celeste was fiddling with the height of her mic stand when she noticed this, "what are you doing?"

"Can't feel restricted in any way when I'm playing", replied Chad, as he took off his trousers and piled his clothes neatly beside him, "your skin needs to be able to breathe during a performance", he now only had on a pair of skimpy tight trunks that bulged in all the right places. You'd swear a baby elephant was trying to push its face through a white cloth.

Jamie was standing near the stage. She'd been trying to get off with Father Jessop, but to no avail. Didn't matter how much she firmly rubbed his sweaty thigh, he still wouldn't get hard, and if he was getting a boner, then it wasn't showing. Neither option was a good thing in her opinion. So when she seen Chad stripping off onstage, Jamie quickly lost interest in the young priest and turned her attentions to Chad. He definitely had a cock worth trying to stand to attention and a body to match. All she had to do now was get his attention somehow.

Father Jessop was delighted to be left alone, yet he still felt a little rejected at how quickly Jamie had moved on to another man.

"Hi everyone", Celeste announced into the mic, "my name is Celeste. Some of you might even know my films. But years ago I started off as a singer. I used to go by the name Heavenly Celeste", a cheer went up from a single man at the back of the room. Celeste pointed in his general direction, "thank you sir. As I was saying, I started out as a singer, and unfortunately due to dwindling sales, I gave it all up for acting. But singing with the legend the Mushy Pea has touched me in ways that I didn't expect", she pointed at the bar where the Mushy Pea was asleep over the counter, "that man awoke something in me and I'd like to share it with all of you. She glanced back at her lack of musicians before taking to the mic again, "unfortunately I'm short a bass and rhythm guitarist, and someone who can play the keyboard and audio backing tracks. Anyone out there that might be able to help me out?"

Three hands shot up from the crowd. It was the O'Malley brothers and sister. Fifteen, sixteen and seventeen years of age. They were in a band called Black Faith. Playing mostly nineties rock songs and some of their own stuff. Heather was the lead singer and guitarist, Barry was the bassist and sang lead on some of their songs, while Jeff was the eldest of them and normally played drums, but he could play the piano if needed for a particular song.

Celeste offered the three of them up onstage and explained what she wanted them to do, before she went back to the mic again, "looks like I have a band. Now all

I need is my singing partner for the first song. Would you like to come up and help me Marcus?"

Marcus glanced up like a deer in headlights. He was lost for words by the offer, and it didn't help that everyone was now looking his way.

Carla knew Marcus better than most, so pulled him to his feet before he had a chance to overthink things too much, "come on and get your ass up on that stage. Think of it this way, at least it might counteract the damage that our video caused"

Marcus couldn't dispute her possible outcome and let himself be guided to the stage as everyone cheered him on. He clambered up beside Celeste and tried not to look at the large crowd staring back at him.

"This is my beautiful and wonderful husband Marcus everybody", Celeste announced. This was followed by a big cheer from the crowd. Celeste continued, "I'm so lucky to have this man in my life. He's my rock, my soulmate, and we all need that type of person to help us get through some of the tougher times in life we all experience. Just a pity that we can sometimes take them for granted. I'm guilty of that and I'm sure a lot of youse can say the same thing", she picked up another microphone and handed it to Marcus, before addressing him directly, "some of my happiest moments with you was when you helped me practice my lyrics for American Idiot the musical. I didn't get the role, but none of that mattered, because I still had those fond memories of us, to look back on. Let's relieve those special times for everyone here"

Before Marcus had time to protest, Celeste signalled the band to start and Tory broke into the opening guitar chords of 21 guns by Green Day. It wasn't the normal version of the song, but the one from the stage musical. Celeste sang the opening lyrics in this operatic singing voice, that few had ever had the pleasure of hearing. Soon it was Marcus's turn to sing and he came in on the heavy drum beating of Chad, who was unknowingly drawing all the eyes of most of the women in the room. Even some of the men.

Gary and Lucas arrived back while all this was going on.

Lucas briefly stood still to listen to Marcus singing, "I didn't know your brother could sing"

"I didn't either", replied Gary, as he searched for his mother in the crowd. He soon spotted her sitting with Carla and rushed over, dragging Lucas by the hand behind him. They then took a seat at the round table, "Take it I missed a lot while I was gone", Gary definitely wasn't expecting to find this scene when he came back.

"They're only getting started", replied Carla, who was half shot already on vodka and whiskey shorts.

But Margaret was more interested in something else, "where did you disappear to Lucas?"

"Had to go deal with something", Lucas lied.

"Did you two had a row", Margaret wasn't stupid and she'd dealt with their little falling outs in the past.

"Nothing we couldn't work through", Gary replied, as he flashed a smile at Lucas.

"That's good", Margaret's eyes wandered back to Celeste and Marcus's performance onstage. So Gary and Lucas did the same.

"Thank you everybody", Celeste announced to the crowd as they finished their first song. She then turned to Marcus, "wanna do the Pink song?"

Marcus really didn't, but he just said yes for a peaceful life.

Celeste instructed the band and Jeff broke into give me just a reason, on the keyboard. Tory and Heather supplied backing vocals once again.

Dolly was standing near the door with Cilla and Frank. Frank was fast asleep in a large armchair that someone had dragged in from the corridor outside. He had taken a lot of painkillers for his back, after he'd fallen into the grave, and now they had finally caught up with him, along with the large amount of alcohol he had recently consumed.

"Turned out a good night", Cilla had kind of forgot herself in the fun of the whole night.

"Do you think?", Dolly replied sarcastically.

Cilla noticed her mistake, "sorry about that sis"

"No, don't being worrying", Dolly dismissed her sister's worries with a wave of her hand, "it has been a good night, and everyone here is enjoying themselves. Why should I expect everyone to be as miserable as I feel right now"

Cilla noticed a load of people wandering in the main door. They were all dressed up in suits and fancy dresses, "who the hell are this lot?"

"Can I help you?", Dolly asked one of the well dressed women.

"We were next door at a wedding and we heard the music", the well dressed woman glanced around the room, "sounds like you're having a better time in here than we're having. Is it a birthday party?"

"No, it's a funeral", even Dolly was struggling to believe it herself, "but you're more than welcome to come in and join the party"

The well dressed woman was shocked at first, but that soon turned to delight as her and her wedding party joined in with the mourners.

Cilla shook her head, "this definitely is one fucked up day"

"Ain't that the fucking truth", replied Dolly.

Celeste finished her duet with Marcus and the crowd cheered. The members of Black Faith were loving the unexpected concert they were now taking part in. Their mother videoing the whole lot, as she planned to post it on social media later that day.

Jamie was hanging around the front of the stage as she stalked her prey. Chad was unaware of her constant eye contact. The sweat constantly dripping from his naked torso.

"Can my beautiful husband get another big cheer?", Celeste held Marcus's hand up in the air and the crowd cheered again, including Gary and Lucas, who had just arrived in. Celeste then turned to her husband, "love you so much"

"I love you too", Marcus replied.

They kissed passionately in front of everyone and the crowd cheered again. Marcus then made his exit from the stage and Celeste went back into concert mode, breaking into lonely boy by the Black Keys. She didn't even bother changing the lyrics from boy to girl. Celeste always felt it was wrong to change lyrics just to suit the singer. Probably why her cover of insane in the brain went down so poorly with the public.

After that, Celeste started into walk like an Egyptian and the crowd was out on the dance floor that was directly in front of the stage. Someone had turned on the underfloor lighting and each small panel of the dance floor was changing to different colours every second.

Sophie and Ellis finally came back from their private chat, to find the party in full swing. Since both of them were of a younger age, they could see the significance of having Heavenly Celeste performing a private concert for them, so they dragged Dolly and Cilla out onto the dance floor, and began to boogie the night away. Both daughters knowing that their father would have loved all this.

This went on for the next two hours. More and more people arriving in from the wedding in the next room. Even some of the reporters and photographers had snuck in, and were shocked to find a mini concert taking place.

Celeste kept the mood high for her entire performance. Never giving the crowd an opportunity to rest, as she went from one dance floor classic to another. She loved the oldies. The sweat was dripping down her toned body. Only regret Celeste had, was that she was not wearing any underwear. Her tight dress kept riding up high on her thighs. Probably explained why all the young teenage boys were standing along the front of the stage.

Unfortunately the time ran out on the use of the musical instruments and Celeste had to bring the concert to an end. She wiped her sweaty hair from her face as she addressed the crowd, "sorry folks, but we have to bring this all to an end now"

The crowd booed and groaned quietly.

"But I'm gonna do one more song for you", Celeste announced through the mic, "and since we're in Ireland, I think it should be an Irish classic"

The band then broke into dreams by the Cranberries. The crowd went wild as Tory supported Celeste on the high notes. The concert ended with a big cheer from the crowd.

Celeste looked out across all the clapping people and soaked up the atmosphere. It was there and then that she decided to go back into music once more. Maybe even release a double sided album of eighties and nineties covers.

Chapter Thirty Six

The next morning, a lot of them woke up to a life a little less ordinary, or just a nice break from the norm.

Bernard had awoken in a strange bedroom with Ellen on one side of him, with only her red shoes on, and Cilla on the other. He knew their had been sex involved with both women, but he couldn't quite remember it.

While poor Frank woke up in an empty function room, after the painkillers had worn off.

Jamie, Carla, Tory and Chad had spent the night together in one of the Gresham's fancier bedrooms. First one awake was Jamie. To be honest, she hadn't slept all night. She had finally gotten her hands on, the Chad, as she liked to call him. Definitely a story to tell her friends. It was also Jamie's first foursome, but she felt it was for the best to leave out the part of the story were another woman had licked her out, when she was recounting her tale to her friends. As for the others, they'd all lost count on how many foursomes they had already.

Spencer didn't go home to his wife. He'd decided that he had to move on with his life and so did Michelle. Thankfully Margaret was more than happy to invite him into her bed, were she blew his mind on several occasions that night. He'd never gotten a blowjob before, off a woman that could take all her teeth out first.

Dolly, Sophie and Ellis had decided to go home that night. They'd all gotten into their pyjamas and sat around the sitting room with glasses of wine, while they talked fondly about Mattie and how they all missed him.

Eu-Meh and her kids had been escorted home by a very drunk Mushy Pea. By morning he had already offered to marry the young woman and look after her family. Just a pity he couldn't remember making such an offer, when he finally woke up the next day.

Gary, Lucas and Aisling had all gone back to Gary's apartment and carried on drinking and taking drugs. They talked about old times, and when Aisling passed out on the couch, Gary put a blanket over her, before the two men retired to his bedroom. Neither of them knowing what the future had in store for them, but neither caring either.

Black Faith woke up the next day to the offer of an album deal. Their sudden breakout fame on social media had took the younger generation of Ireland by storm. Their new agent telling them that they were gonna be the next U2.

Rory and Katie hadn't retired to anywhere that night. Spending the whole time walking around the busier streets of the city. Having coffee in McDonald's at four in the morning. Kissing under the spire, until finally putting the young woman on the seven o'clock bus back to her home. Rory felt young again as he waved her off.

He just hoped Katie wouldn't lose interest in him too quickly.

Finally, Marcus and Celeste had retired to the penthouse suite after their busy day, and made love in a way that took both of them by surprise. Their love was stronger than before and both of them knew it. Before they fell asleep that night, the loving couple had planned to renew their wedding vows in Ireland the following year. A big lavish castle wedding in the midlands of Ireland. They also both agreed that Father Jessop wouldn't be officiating the ceremony.

Chapter Thirty Seven

It was ten to three. Margaret liked to be early for official appointments. Helped her feel the vibe that was hanging in the air before whatever happened. Today was no different. She'd been summoned to the solicitor's office of one Andrew Taylor. A man who had couriered out a load of official paperwork for her to sign the previous morning. Freshly printed documents that signed away any rights she may have had to Mattie's fortune.

It was easy enough. Margaret had been living for decades without the help of Mattie's money. Why change all that now?. She had a simple enough life and was happy with her lot. Soon Margaret would have to move out of the Gresham and go back to squatting in that drug den of a house again. She'd already lied to her sons about where she was moving to in a few days. Marcus believed his mother was moving in with Gary for a while, and had gone back to America that morning, with Celeste and the rest of their entourage.

But Margaret didn't want to be bothering Gary as he had just moved Lucas into his place, and they seemed to be getting on great. Margaret didn't want to get in the way of all that. So she decided to say nothing to Gary either, and just disappear off back to her squat when her time was up in the Gresham. Margaret hoped that both her boys would soon forget about her, and then they could all move on with their lives individually.

Margaret pushed the intercom button that was next to the large wooden door, and stood back to admire the townhouse once more. It was just off Saint Stephen's Green, but probably still cost as much. The door buzzed open and Margaret entered a large hallway that still looked like it was in the original Georgian style with its use of timber and high ceilings

A young redhead woman in a business suit stepped out from a room further down the hall. She greeted Margaret politely and ushered her into another room further along, all the time apologising for what would be a few minutes of a delay. Margaret decided not to point out that she was the one who was early.

Margaret stepped into another room that was like some kind of old fashioned library, with its old smelly books and wooden shelves on every wall. There was two large leather couches in the centre, both facing each other. Eu-Meh was sat on one of them, and her face lit up when she seen Margaret.

"Hi Margaret", said Eu-Meh in her usual broken English, "I did not know that you'd be here"

Margaret sat down on the opposite couch, "only got the phone call this morning. Do you know what this is all about?"

Eu-Meh shook her head, "only was told this morning as well. Did not want to come, but my parents insisted that I should"

"Has to be something to do with Dolly", that much was obvious to Margaret.

Suddenly two bookshelves beside them, slid sideways in opposite directions to reveal another office. The redhead in the business suit had been the one who had opened them. At a large desk sat a balding old man in a suit that had seen better days. Dolly was standing next to the desk and walked out to meet the two other wives of Mattie Jenkins.

"I'm glad you both could come", Dolly shook both women's hands politely.

"What's all this about Dolly?", Margaret was suspicious as she entered the next room and took a seat.

Eu-Meh sat in the chair beside Margaret and said nothing.

Dolly stood next to the desk in her high heels and tight blue dress, that showed off the body that her plastic surgeon had given her, "we've all been screwed over by Mattie in someway or another. You getting the worst of it Margaret by having to hold onto such a damaging secret all these years. You could have destroyed my marriage at anytime. Left my kids with nothing if you chose to do so. But you didn't, and then you signed the paperwork yesterday to secure mine and the twin's future"

"How are Sophie and Ellis after the other night?", Margaret had been aware of some going ons with the twin's love life.

Dolly sat on the corner of the desk, "they're okay. Both of them are back living with me. It's nice having them home for now. Hopefully they'll both get their lives back on track in time. But that's not why I brought you here today", Dolly stood back up from the edge of the desk and fixed her dress. She turned to Eu-Meh, "it's not fair that Mattie led you and your family on like he did. You and your kids thought that you had security for the rest of your lives, and he's now left you without that. That's why I'm signing over to you, the entire building that your family's massage parlour is in. I've also arranged a special account for your three kids, to make sure all of them will get the best education possible. If they wanna go to Trinity College, that's all sorted"

Eu-Meh was lost for words at first, but soon found her timid voice once more, "thank you Dolly. You are so kind to us", there was tears coming to the young Chinese woman's eyes.

"I'm just trying to make up for the mistakes that our husband made throughout his life", Dolly hadn't told anyone, but she'd gotten her solicitor to complete a rather thorough investigation into the life of her dead husband. To see was there anymore skeletons rattling around his rather large wardrobe.

"I hope I'm not getting a massage parlour as well?",
Margaret joked. Her wrists weren't what they used to be
for dishing out happy endings on a daily basis.

Dolly couldn't help but laugh slightly, "no, I'm not
giving you a massage parlour", she picked up a few
pieces of paper from the desk and handed them to
Margaret.

Margaret quickly noticed that it was one of those
pamphlets that estate agents have to advertise different
properties. This one in particular was for a fancy looking
apartment near the centre of town. She stared up at Dolly
in confusion, "what's this all about?"

"It's your new home if you're willing to accept it", Dolly
was smiling from ear to ear.

Margaret studied the paperwork in her hands a little
more carefully, before staring up at Dolly once more,
"do you own this place?"

"No", Dolly replied, "but you will, if you accept my
offer. Only thing it will cost you is a thousand a year in
maintenance fees and that's that"

Margaret figured there would be a downer in all this,
"wouldn't even have that kind of money to keep a place
going"

"Not any more", Dolly held up a check for Margaret to
see.

Margaret noticed there was a lot of zeros after the number five. Way too many to count easily, "fifty thousand!", she announced with delight.

"Five hundred thousand", Dolly corrected, "five hundred thousand euros. That should keep you living pretty damn comfortably for the rest of your days"

Margaret was lost for words as she studied the cheque once more, and then the pamphlet for the lavish apartment, "I don't know what to say"

"You don't have to say anything", Dolly pushed a form across the desk, along with a gold pen, "all you have to do is sign this piece of paper", she pulled out a set of keys from her handbag, "and all this is yours"

"You sure about this?", Margaret asked.

"I've never been as sure about anything in all my life", replied Dolly, "now please just sign it and we can all move on from this terrible week"

Margaret signed the paperwork in seven separate places and then Eu-Meh did the same on a different piece of paperwork. The young redhead then showed the three women out and Eu-Meh said her goodbyes before hurrying off down the street. She couldn't wait to tell her parents the good news.

Dolly and Margaret stood there briefly for a few moments, at the bottom of the steep steps that led up to the solicitor's office. Neither knew what to say to the other at first. Today seemed like a kind of final goodbye for both of them.

"So what's gonna happen with you now?", Margaret asked, "any plans for the future?"

"I'm gonna sell up a lot of the properties and businesses. Keep the shares and maybe move abroad. Too much being said behind my back these days. Not even behind my back. The media had a fucking field day with Spencer, and Mattie's head", Dolly lit up a much needed cigarette.

"Surprised they were allowed to put that photo up uncensored", Margaret got an urge for a cigarette as well and lit up one of her own, "you back on the fags again?"

"Never fucking off them", Dolly replied through a big puff of smoke, "just can't be bothered trying to hide it anymore. Can't exactly damage my image any further"

"Wanna go get a drink somewhere?. Talk about things", Margaret held up the check for half a million euros, "feeling a little flush today"

"Fuck it", Margaret replied, as she fired away the last of her cigarette, "I know a good place that does bottomless Prosecco at this time of day"

"Lead the way", Margaret replied, as she bent her arm as an offer for Dolly to interlock her own with it.

Dolly did just that, and the two women strolled off down the quiet street. Arm in arm and ready for anything the world might throw at them.

Printed in Great Britain
by Amazon

87184973R00183